Magdalena's Demons

A Mystical Romance

Pamella Bowen

GREEN AND PURPLE
PUBLISHING

Magdalena's Demons

ISBN 978-1-950190-08-9

Green and Purple Publishing

California, USA

www.greenandpurplepublishing.com

This is a work of fiction. Though actual persons who once lived or scriptural characters may be portrayed, their thoughts and actions in this work are the invention of the author and should not be taken to be factual.

Dedicated to Don, Amy, and Pippa who, together, taught me to let go.

Acknowledgments

Thanks to Eroica Woodruff who loaned me her name and her opinion on the story and style. Thanks to the members of the online Mary Magdalene course taught by Cynthia Bourgeault who encouraged me and made me think. Thanks to Therese Kay Creative for the text design.

Though this fictional work is my own invention, I am grateful for the inspiration three books gave me:

Cynthia Bourgeault's *The Meaning of Mary Magdalene: Discovering the Woman at the Heart of Christianity*. Shambhala, 2010.

Karen L. King's *The Gospel of Mary of Magdala: Jesus and the First Woman Apostle*. Polebridge, 2003.

Meggan Watterson's *Mary Magdalene Revealed: The First Apostle, Her Feminist Gospel and the Christianity We Haven't Tried Yet*. Hay House, 2019.

Chapter 1

River

"Zeno, please prepare Jael for riding. We have an important meeting down by the river," Magdalena called to her manservant.

"Shall I pack you water and food, my lady?"

"Yes, enough for both of us." She braided her long dark hair and covered it with a veil. Since she would be riding her donkey, she couldn't wear her finest outer robe, but she made sure she looked clean and presentable. She perfumed herself with cinnamon and clove, her preferred scent. If her vision of the night before boded well, she would see something, or someone, remarkable today, and it would change her life.

After covering the six miles from Magdala to the river, she and Zeno crested the high bank above the Jordan to look down on a large crowd assembled near the water. The whole town had been buzzing with the news that John the Weird Prophet would be baptizing again today, and when she dreamed of the scene last night, she knew she had to be there. She, of course, would not be dunked in that muddy water, but she didn't want to miss anything that could pull her up out of her darkness.

When she looked down, John was standing in the water talking to a long-haired man, with his blessing hand on the man's head. Then he tipped the man backward into the brown water and pulled him back up. When Magdalena saw him arise from the river, she knew he was the One, the person whom she was meant to see.

Just then, the One and John looked up at the sky, and her eyes turned skyward, too. None of the others by the water or on the tall bank seemed to notice anything. But Magdalena did. The grayish clouds that had kept the day cool by shading the river suddenly broke apart, and a solid beam of sun arrowed down, shining a circle around John and the One. They glowed in a light she had never seen before, in reality or in dream. It was yellow like sunshine, but greenish edges scintillated on the river's surface around it. Then she heard a deep-voiced rumble among the clouds. She thought the rumble said, "This is my Beloved Child. I am pleased with him."

Below her, John's mouth gaped in awe, and the One bowed his streaming head. The crowd chatted and moved about as if nothing had happened. Only she and John and the One had heard the voice and seen the light.

Magdalena kept her eyes on the One as he wrapped his robe over his dripping tunic and bent to pull on his sandals. John came out of the water with him, embraced him, and lifted his arm in farewell as the One climbed the bank where Magdalena stood. He looked up and caught her eye. Instantly, she felt the thrill of recognition run through her. She knew this slim, otherworldly man, but she had never met him, unless in a vision. Just then, a rock slipped from under the man's foot, and he started to topple. Magdalena reached out her hand and grabbed his wrist. He looked up into her face, smiled and said, "Thank you, Sister."

As she pulled him up the bank, she looked boldly into his eyes and said, "I'm called Magdalena."

The One smiled and said, "Yes, but your name is Mary."

Then he passed her by and continued away from the river with several friends. Magdalena could still feel the warmth of his body in her hand, even after she had released him. She looked to see if her hand were glowing green like the circle of sunlight on the river, but it looked normal. The encounter, though, was far from normal. She had to follow him.

"Come on, Zeno, don't lose sight of him. Hurry up. Fetch Jael."

"But, my lady, you can't just go after him like that."

"Oh, yes, Zeno, I can and I must. And you're coming too."

Magdalena had sharp eyes, in her head and in her heart. She would have made a good hunter if she had been born a man. As it was, she used her heart's eyes as most women do, to see into women's business: love, family, household, and healing. Today, though, she needed the sharp eyes in her head to keep the One within her ken but distant. She didn't want to be seen following him. As they left the hubbub of the riverside, she realized that Jael's footfalls and snorts could be heard, and she dismounted.

"I'm going to follow on foot, Zeno. Wait here for me to return with news."

"No, my lady. I will tie Jael to a bush and hide her. Her safety is less important than yours. I am a silent tracker.

3

I'm coming with you."

Magdalena didn't argue. After all the years Zeno had served her, she trusted and relied on him. When her husband Tiras died, she offered to free Zeno and buy his passage back to Byzantium where he had been purchased as a eunuch slave. Zeno refused, wishing to continue to serve her in Magdala. Now he was a free servant, paid and honored by his mistress for his dedicated service.

Silently, they followed the One away from the river into the dry brown hills. The clouds had evaporated leaving the sun beating on hot sand and scraggly bushes. Magdalena pulled her veil up to shade her head, keeping close to Zeno who chose a route behind tamarisk trees and rocky outcrops. If the One turned to look back, his pursuers would be hidden. Finally, they saw him enter a cave partway up the side of a dry hillside. They waited, but he didn't emerge.

"Zeno, I will be safe here. Go find Jael and return to Magdala for supplies. I will not leave this spot. Bring my traveling tent, water and food, blankets, and anything else you think we need."

"I will bring my dagger and short sword, but my lady, are we going to camp out here?"

"Yes, dear Zeno, until the One comes out of his cave, I will watch."

"It will be dark soon."

"Yes. Leave me some food, water, and Jael's blanket."

"I will also leave you my mantle, my lady."

"Thank you, Zeno. I will see you tomorrow, and we will have an adventure together."

Zeno smiled. His mistress's brightness eased his heart. Maybe she was coming out of her despair. He crept away quietly the way they had come.

Magdalena's camp across the valley from the cave was partly hidden by a large rock. She could see the cave's mouth, but she could not hear movement above the strong winds that blew almost constantly. As darkness fell, she saw a glow coming out of the cave. The color of the light was natural and homely, like a small camp cooking fire. Happy that the One had light and warmth to keep him well during the night, she pulled Zeno's mantle around her shoulders, sitting in the darkness. Praying in her heart for the man to be safe, Magdalena fell asleep on her donkey's blanket.

Detailed and prolonged, the dream she had, curled up in the dark, would never thereafter leave her memory. She stood looking across a valley at a bright rainbow. The colors shone vibrant and alive until a dark cloud appeared above, shooting out lightning bolts in a torrent. One of the bolts struck the rainbow directly in the middle, splitting it into two ribbons. One ribbon carried the cool colors of blue, green, and violet; the other carried the warm colors of red, orange, and yellow. When the split occurred, a cry like that of a banshee echoed through the air, and in her mind Magdalena smelled sulfur. Rising up into the sky, the two ribbons of color floated away in separate directions to circle the earth, one traveling to the east and the other to the west. A tender yearning filled Magdalena's heart and she wanted to sob, but couldn't. She knew that the ribbons were trying to find each other again, to reunite into a full rainbow, but their frantic search was thwarted by some evil. The towns scattered on the earth below had lost their color and life. Gray and brown tinged the trees, the oceans, and the birds of the air.

She woke when she heard Zeno's footfalls approaching.

"My goodness, Zeno, I didn't expect you until after midday."

"I traveled all night, my lady, not wanting to leave you alone too long."

"God bless you, my friend. Once we set up the tent, you can sleep. I have had a good night full of dreams."

"Has the man left his cave?"

"No. He had a fire that went out after a few hours. The wind died down, and I have heard nothing."

"Let me serve you some breakfast, my lady." And Zeno set about making the camp livable, feeding his mistress on dates, cheese, and bread. Then he retired to the tent while Magdalena kept her vigil across the distance.

During the day, the One carried on a strange ritual life. He emerged from the cave's mouth, raised his arms to the sky and said some sort of prayer. Then he walked in a rough circle around the valley before the cave, stopping to observe any plant or animal life he encountered. Magdalena's sharp eyes sometimes caught him moving his lips, shaking his head, or gesturing with his hands as if he were speaking to an invisible companion. Then he would sit in whatever shade he could find, under a scrubby tree or the shadow of a rock. Still and silent, he sat for a long time, his palms open on his knees. Magdalena thought she could never sit still that long. If her bottom or her back didn't act up, her mind was bound to stir her. But the One sat contentedly without moving, and when he got up he seemed refreshed and energetic. When he disappeared into the cave, Magdalena imagined he was napping. In the cool of the late afternoon, he would prostrate himself face-down on an open area of sand at the cave's mouth and lie there, motionless. When he arose, he brushed sand from his face and saluted the heavens again with upraised hands.

"Does he have any water?" Zeno asked.

"He walked here empty-handed. Unless he had stocked the cave in advance, I don't think so."

"Should we take him food and water? I could leave it outside his cave. He will think the angels brought it." Zeno smiled at his mistress.

Magdalena smiled back. Zeno had such a good heart. "I don't think so. Whatever he has in mind, I trust he knows what he is doing. If it goes on many days, we may do what you suggest. These ascetic fanatics sometimes overdo their privations. I promise we won't let him starve."

That evening as dusk faded into night, Magdalena saw a shadow like a bat or an ink spill swooping over the cave. It fluttered about the hillside, poked a tendril of black into the cave, then flew away over the valley. A sound like a flag flapping in the wind accompanied the shadow.

"Zeno, did you see that?"

"No, my lady. What was it?"

"I don't know, but it turned my blood to ice. We must pray all night for the One."

"Yes, we can take it in shifts. I will go first. You get some rest. I will keep watch and pray."

For the next two nights, Magdalena saw the shadow visit the cave. Each time, she felt its presence as evil, and she watched at sunrise for the One to emerge, fearful that he might have died in the night. She and Zeno kept the prayer vigil. On the morning after the third night, the One was late coming out of the cave, and when he walked out, he staggered. He lay face down on his prayer spot without taking his morning walk around the valley. Magdalena's heart sank, and she felt herself called to his side.

"Come on, Zeno. Grab the water and food. We can't keep away."

By the time the two watchers had crossed the deserted distance, the One had gotten up on hands and knees and crawled back into the cave's mouth. He was sitting cross-legged with his head sagging down on his chest when Magdalena approached. As her feet scraped the sandy entrance, he looked up and said,

"Mary, you came."

Then he sank into a delirium in which he thrashed on the cave floor, calling out in agitated words she and Zeno couldn't understand. He was shaking, so Zeno put a blanket over him, and Mary held the water skin to his lips. Eventually, he calmed down and slept. The watchers set up their vigil in the cave mouth, looking back in the direction of their own camp. From here, their tent was invisible. Why had the One said, "Mary, you came" as if he knew she was out there, watching over him? How had he known her birth name, Mary, when they had never met before the day at the river? She never called herself Mary. Such a common name. She had always called herself Magdalena. Questions like these tormented her mind, but her heart was at peace. She was watching over the One she was connected to by an invisible but strong tie linking her heart to his, across any distance, across any time.

Chapter 2

Wilderness

Magdalena realized she had fallen asleep when the One's voice said, "So why did you name your donkey Jael?" He was sitting cross-legged on the cave floor near her, and he looked at her with a slight smile.

"How do you know her name?"

"I know a lot of things."

"Then why ask me?"

"I want to hear you tell about it."

"Well, Jael is a spunky woman in the scriptures, and she's a spunky donkey."

"I thought maybe it was because you hated your father and your husband."

Magdalena, speechless, demurred. He looked quizzical. Finally, she relented.

"I did hate them, and I often fantasized about driving a nail through their heads when they were asleep. I confess it. My father forced me to marry Tiras when I was very young. He was old, ugly and smelled horrid, but he was rich and influential. He was cruel to me and cruel to Zeno. All Tiras cared about was money. He traveled the world trading in spices and herbs. I was glad when he traveled because he left us alone."

"Is that when you slept with Jubal?"

Magdalena blushed. "Yes. He was an artisan hired to embellish our house with carving on the doorposts, lintel, and roof beams. Just Tiras showing off his wealth. Jubal was young, strong, and beautiful. You can guess the rest."

"I know you conceived Jubal's child. How did you keep from conceiving with Tiras?"

"I drank laserwort tea every day when Tiras was home, but not when he was away. I was overjoyed to know I was with child. I thought I would at least have someone to love me. But she died in her first week. After that, my life went dark."

"Yes, I see that you have many darknesses in you, Mary. Tell me how Tiras died."

"Robbers set upon him on his way home from a party where he was furthering his business interests. They stabbed him and took his purse. The old fool was too proud to ask for help at any house and tried to walk home. He died in the road."

Zeno interrupted, coming in from the bright outdoors, "My lady, I am going to retrieve Jael and fetch food. Have you any special requests?"

"Oh, yes," and Magdalena arose and stepped out to give Zeno her secret shopping list. When she returned, she feared to meet the One's eye.

"Mary, I didn't ask you about your life to shame you. Your answers show me your wounds that need healing. Will you let me help you clear some of the darkness from your mind?"

"Maybe. If you heal me, can I follow you?" He smiled.

"You could follow me anyway. Are you willing?"

"Yes, but what can you do for me, short of an exorcism?"

The One smiled. "People toss around a lot of words carelessly without knowing what they mean. Your demons are not the kind that need exorcising. They stem from illusions you have been carrying in your mind all your life. The first step is silence. I want you to pray with me in silence."

"Not that sitting in one place forever, not moving."

"Yes, that's it."

"I don't think I can do it."

"Just try with me. The power and love of God will wash through you and take away some of the darkness." And he showed her how to sit still and let thoughts go past, allowing the quiet to calm her heart. When he called her from her reverie, she felt comforted. The depth she had reached reminded her of how she felt when she had a vision or dream. If silent prayer tapped into the same energies as her visions, she would gladly continue the practice. She smiled at him.

"That was wonderful. Can we do it again?"

"We can do it several times a day."

"Will you teach Zeno, too?"

"Of course. It's open to all willing to try it. With some it works, with others it doesn't. It depends on eyes to see and ears to hear."

"I didn't hear or see anything. My eyes were shut."

The One smiled again. He reached out his hand and caressed her face. "Dear Mary," he said. His touch electrified her, and she struggled with feelings of desire and contentment. What was she meant to feel in the presence of this man? Her internal voice said, "Love."

As Magdalena and the One walked around the valley, she pointed out all the plants she knew to be useful for medicine or cooking.

"How did you learn all this lore?" he asked.

"My mother was a healer and taught me the basics. Then I learned more in the spice business with Tiras. Most people look at the wilderness as a dead thing, but it is full of life and healing. Every plant on earth has some purpose. God wouldn't have wasted time making something useless." She didn't see the amused smile on his face at that remark. Just then, they noticed a dusty wisp arising across the valley and Zeno appeared leading Jael, laden with packs and bags.

"Oh, here they come with our dinner!" Magdalena cried, and hurried toward them. Zeno unloaded carpets, wine and water skins, cushions, oil lamps, dishes, pots, the traveling tent, and sacks containing cheese, bread, and all the special items Magdalena had asked for, except apples. There were no apples to be found.

"Here, my lord, take a seat," Zeno offered, putting down a cushion on the cave floor. "We will set out a feast for you."

On a striped cloth, Magdalena and Zeno laid out bowls of grapes, pomegranates, figs, and raisins. Beside the wine, a jug of milk and a jar of honey stood by two footed cups. Magdalena lit the lamps, as the cave was darkening with the sinking sun.

"Are you planning to seduce me tonight?" he asked, giving her an arch look.

"Why do you say that?" she asked, embarrassed.

"These are foods for a love feast, picked with care from *Song of Songs*, the most sensuous poem in the scripture. Except the apples."

She looked down, shamefaced. Of course he had read the foods precisely and stripped away the veil on her intention. "I don't know what to say."

"Come, Mary, no secrets between us. You are the soul of my soul, and we must be one. However, those powers that entrap you are a hurdle we must overcome or remove. Let us eat the love feast you have prepared, let us share our hearts openly. But no seduction. We will be married first."

Zeno's mouth dropped open. Such unrestrained speech between unmarried people was not at all proper. Magdalena looked deeply into the eyes of her beloved, accepting his proposal, and handed him a bowl of dates. They ate in joyful silence while Zeno set up the tent outside the cave mouth. He expected his mistress to sleep in her tent, with himself on watch. In the end, Zeno slept in the tent. Magdalena slept in the arms of her beloved on the carpet in the cave. It was the most natural and peaceful sleep she had ever slept.

───────── • ─────────

Silent prayer three times a day, once in the cave, once under the huge acacia tree that somehow found water under the dry sand, and once in the shadow of the rock, formed part of the daily ritual. Magdalena and the One dined on the seductive foods she had brought him, along with the homely bread and cheese. They walked hand in hand around the valley, learning about the flora and greeting any lizards or foxes they saw. But most of their day they talked. Magdalena shared more of her life, the One told her what he had experienced when the inky shadow visited the cave, and they worked together on the demons.

Under the shade of the rock, he asked Magdalena to

close her eyes and imagine.

"Mary, in your mind's eye, I want you to see a time when someone made you angry, so angry you wanted to strike out at that person."

She took a deep breath and let her mind drop into the place she went during silent prayer, the place where her visions arose. She saw Tiras, drunk, pushing Zeno out the door with a curse and raising his stick to beat her across the back as she cowered on the floor.

"Now take all the rage you were feeling and gather it into a ball in the palm of your hand."

She imagined the ball of rage. Just gathering it into one place cleared the air in the scene. She felt the heat of it burning her hand.

"Now squeeze the ball tight." She did. "Now open your hand and give it away, to whoever will take it."

In her mind, she opened her hand and the ball floated up and away. As it arose, her heart lightened.

"Now, look into Tiras's face. Say, 'I forgive you, Tiras.'"

Magdalena had complied easily with all the previous instructions, but she balked at this. She didn't want to forgive Tiras. She hated him, and the ball of rage still burned in her hand, though she had seen it float away. She looked into Tiras's eyes, and the anger she had seen there now looked like fear. Something peeled away from her vision, and she saw his weakness. Then his eyes filled with tears and he said, 'Please forgive me, Magdalena.' Compassion for this suffering old man flooded her heart, and she easily said, 'I forgive you, Tiras.'

When she opened her eyes, the One's eyes held hers, overpowering her with love. Words were beyond her. With her beloved's help, she had exorcised one of her demons. Already she felt reborn, and strong enough to take on the next one. Walking back to the cave, they passed Jael, hitched to a tamarisk tree. Her head was down as she snuffled the dust, searching for an edible sprout.

"Jael, my trusty beast," Magdalena said, laying her hand on the donkey's neck, "I think you need a new name." Jael raised her head. "You are now called Sophia." The donkey let out a loud bray that drove the crows out of a nearby thorn tree. The One laughed.

"She likes her new name. Wisdom drives out rage. I think she is relieved," he said.

"Well, I am definitely relieved. Thank you, my love," Magdalena said. "What name may I call you?"

"My birth name is Yeshua." And from that day, Magdalena called her beloved Yeshua. Others called him Master, Rabbi, and Teacher. But she called him Yeshua, my love, dear one, and later husband. He called her Mary.

Yeshua helped her take on one demon per day. She called it her daily exorcism. The depressing darkness that overcame her when her daughter died had led to other traps, like inertia. Some days she was unable to rise from her bed, and she spent till sundown under covers, crying and wishing for death. Sometimes, she took drugs like blue water lily in wine to make herself forget and dull the pain. Zeno had hidden the wine flask, but she had found it again and again, trying to end her own suffering. On days when she could stir herself, she would stare out the window, watching other women in the town who had living babies, carrying them on their hips as they haggled in the market. She envied those women. She yearned for what she couldn't have, seeing no value in her life since it was not that life. In her ignorance, she blamed everyone else: her mother for dying and leaving her to her father's disposal, her father for selling her into marital bondage, her husband for beating her, her lover for giving her false hope, her daughter for dying. And the blame stirred her rage, and her rage made her want to dull the pain with food, wine, drugs, whatever she could find. These were her demons. They were not horned devils from an underground hell; they were creations of her own unhappiness that had taken over her life, oppressing and enslaving her. As she prayed and worked through them with Yeshua, their grip on her loosened, and her mood lightened. Instead of blaming all the people in her life, she forgave them, one by one, day after day.

One night she dreamed that she awoke in the desert cave and walked to the mouth to look upon the day. A forest of green blocked her view. Sycamores, pines, and cedars reached up into a blue sky flashing with red and yellow songbirds. A waterfall's roar drew her eyes to the mountain crag across the valley. Between banks thronged with greenery, a wide river flowed under stone bridges. Orchards and vineyards swept up both sides of the living valley. Suddenly, she realized she was naked, but she was not ashamed. Rather, she wanted to run into the valley, feel the sun on her skin, and leap into the river. Her mind broke the spell by telling her the vision couldn't last, and the vision faded. At sunup, when she did walk to the cave's mouth, the wilderness had changed. There were no forests or vineyards, but she saw with new eyes the beauty of the barrenness. Everything in creation had beauty. In this wilderness, her beloved had taught her and helped her to let go of her shackles. She had dropped her clothes, woven of pain, anger, and blame, and she yearned to step out naked into the bright world that called to her. Yeshua put his hand on her shoulder.

"Beautiful, isn't it?"

With tears in her eyes, she turned to embrace him, laying her head against his beating heart.

Chapter 3

Cana

Magdalena woke to find Yeshua and Zeno in a serious talk outside the cave. She heard them discussing Sophia, packs, terrain, and routes. Her heart beat faster, knowing that change was about to come.

"May I know the plans?" she asked when her beloved came into the cave.

"We are leaving tomorrow morning early, heading up to Cana. My brother Jude is marrying Nathaniel's sister. All my family and friends will be there. I thought it would be a good time for us to sign a marriage contract."

"Are you sure you want to be betrothed to a widow and an adulteress?"

"Mary, you are not the same woman who walked into this wilderness. Your past errors are washed away in God's forgiveness. Don't you feel that is true?"

"Maybe, but what will your family and others say?" Zeno nodded agreement outside the cave as he listened in.

"The ones who matter will understand, and those who don't may come to understand later. That is no hindrance in my mind."

"Can we just sign the contract quietly? I don't want to steal any joy from your brother's celebration."

"Of course. Our marriage is on a higher plane than my brother's. We don't require the big show and the hilarity. I would like to dance, though. I haven't danced since I first became a man."

"I would love to see you dance, my love. Let me help with the packing." And the day filled with the happy bustle of embarking on a journey.

Since Sophia was carrying most of the baggage, she could carry no passengers. Yeshua, Zeno, and Magdalena walked at a good pace beside her in the morning, but as the sun shone brighter, they slowed to a trudge. Shade was their salvation, and as they neared the river, they gave thanks for water. Magdalena had never been to Cana, but she heard there was a lovely synagogue there. In her mind, the voice of fear and pride started to feed her worries about appearances---her clothes, her age, her reputation, her manner with Yeshua, her arrival with a eunuch servant. But the new Magdalena had tools to deal with that voice. She rolled all these worries into a ball and let them go, floating up into the air where an unseen hand took them from her. Then she was free to look at the green edges of the river, the movement of the water, the wild flowers that sprouted along the road, and the handsome profile of her soon-to-be husband. God and nature were generous, always giving overflowing love and beauty. She had no worries worth thinking about, and she turned her eyes toward Cana.

Had they been able to fly with the crows, they could

have traveled to Cana directly from their wilderness cave over the mountains, but their route took them back down to the shore of the lake and up the western side, passing through Tiberias. A stop in Magdala enabled them to rest, bathe, and unload Sophia. Magdalena's house was large with an ample central courtyard and several surrounding rooms. Yeshua noticed the fine carvings on the woodwork, left by Jubal. Magdalena and Zeno produced a meal while Yeshua ventured into the town to find a messenger he could send to Nathaniel in Cana, letting him know his party would arrive the next day.

"I would like to take a gift to your brother and his bride. Some pickled fish for the feast, our local specialty, or this box of spices, or both!" Yeshua smiled and nodded that both would be welcome. Magdalena had always been tenderhearted, but now her love flowed out in torrents.

———————————— ● ————————————

By the time their little band had covered the ten miles from Magdala to Cana, Sophia carrying a much lighter load, they had missed the early stages of the wedding, and the party was in full swing at Nathaniel's house.

"I will go see the rabbi to let him know we need a marriage contract. Maybe we can sign it tomorrow. Mary, this is my mother, Mary, my brothers James and Joses, and my sisters Susannah and Rhoda. There are more, but you will meet them when I return from the synagogue."

Magdalena stood awkwardly, a stranger among strangers. Mary took her hand and looked into her face, smiling.

"Welcome, Daughter," she said. "I am so glad you finally found my son and me. We have been praying for you to come." And Yeshua's mother took Magdalena in her arms and kissed her cheek. Tears sprang into Magdalena's eyes, and she sobbed. She had not embraced a woman since her mother died. Mary pulled back and smiled at her tearful new daughter, "It's all right, my dear. Loving him is a challenge, but we two are strong. We will stand together." A shiver thrilled up Magdalena's spine; she was sure Mary's words were a prophecy.

By the time Yeshua returned, Joses had whispered in his mother's ear, and Mary frowned. Apparently more guests had arrived than expected or they were guzzling apace, and the wine was running out. When Mary told Yeshua about the problem, he shook his head and said something that caused her to shake hers. Eventually, he shrugged and followed the wine steward off to the kitchen. In a few minutes, plenty of wine—good wine--- was being passed around the room, and the merriment increased. Yeshua's brother Jude and the bride approached Magdalena.

"I hear you are to be our sister. Welcome. I am Jude, and my bride is Eunice."

"I am called Magdalena. Your brother calls me Mary."

"That's wise," said Eunice, "to call yourself something other than Mary. We have so many Marys among us. Magdalena, will you be teaching the women among the followers?"

Magdalena started. "Did the master tell you that?"

"No," said Eunice, "but we women were talking about it. We need a leader who can speak to us of the master's teachings. The men let us listen in, from the back of the room, but we need someone who understands our perspective, who can explain it better. Not to say that the master doesn't speak well, but he is so..."

"...advanced?" Magdalena provided a generous adjective.

Eunice smiled. "Yes, advanced."

Magdalena wondered when and where all this discussion of her role as teacher had taken place. Yes, some of them had seen her at the river when Yeshua was baptized, but no messengers had been sent from the wilderness to the believers in Galilee to update them on her progress. They all seemed to know she was to wed the master, though no announcement had been made. She chose to let the question go. Most of them had welcomed her warmly, so there was no reason to second-guess.

"I will talk to the master about it. I am willing to talk to the sisters about my story and share what he has taught me."

Eunice smiled and embraced her soon-to-be sister-in-law.

"Mary, the rabbi wants to see us today. We need two witnesses. I'll bring Levi and Simon," said Yeshua. "Then we will dance."

The walk from Nathaniel's house to the synagogue was short, and the signing was done quickly. Magdalena received a copy, Yeshua his, and the third the rabbi kept for the synagogue records. Yeshua's brother Simon called her 'sister' and saluted her politely, but Levi looked deep into her eyes. She saw his heart and his kindness there. Perhaps Levi had also learned to let go of his demons, for his true being reached out to hers.

"Levi, will you dance when we return to the wedding?" Magdalena asked.

"I suppose. At least when men dance together, one

man's stumbles can be overlooked."

"And you, Brother?"

"At my little brother's wedding, of course," Simon replied. "And we'd better hurry back, too."

The musicians were already in full voice, and the men had formed up their circle in the middle of the large courtyard. Simon, Levi, and Yeshua broke into the circle and joined in the dance. Watching and clapping to the rhythm, the women stood aside. The swirling and stamping of the men thrilled Magdalena. She had always loved music and could not stand still when people were dancing.

"Come, sisters, let's form our own circle," she said, leading them into the largest room off the courtyard, where they could still hear the music and could dance together privately. Most of the female guests followed her. They were used to meeting separately from the men, and they loved to dance if they got a chance. Joining hands, they circled to the left and then to the right, smiling and laughing and singing.

The hilarity in the women's room rose to a daring peak, and Eunice called out, "Let's go, ladies!" She freed one of her hands and led the chain of women into the courtyard where they formed their circle again, around the circle of men. Some of the men looked offended, but Mother Mary and Nathaniel smiled and laughed. The men's circle was swirling to the right, so Eunice urged the women's circle to the left, and the joyful rings rotated in opposite directions, gaining speed. Suddenly, Magdalena's vision of the rainbow ribbons flashed on her memory, and she saw the warm ribbon as feminine and the cool ribbon as masculine. The vision's message seemed to say that the separation of men and women was part of the world's darkness. Around and around they went, yearning for union but separated by custom. How fitting that she should see this at her in-laws' wedding, on the day she signed her contract to Yeshua. She knew the voice of Love was speaking to her.

Out of breath from dancing and laughing, the dancers broke up and went to fill their cups. There was plenty of the good wine, and someone had opened the large jar of pickled fish she had brought, so they feasted some more. The overflowing food, wine, and jollity assured her that heaven blessed this marriage of Jude and Eunice. She hoped her own would be equally blessed.

Chapter 4

New Moon

"My lady, shall I bring in Keturah to help with the party? She can clean while I prepare the food. Do the women know to bring their own bedding?" Zeno asked.

"Yes, and many of them will be bringing food, so we may need to set up another table."

The new moon was the perfect time for the women followers to come to Magdalena's house. During the light of the full moon, their men went night fishing and needed their spouses at home to help with the catch, but in the dark of the new moon, they didn't go out fishing but listened to the master's teaching. Yeshua and Magdalena had discussed the arrangement, and the three-day women's gathering had become popular with the female followers. The men spent time with the master, and the women came to Magdalena for rest, fellowship, and teaching. Ancient wisdom also said that during the new moon the curtain separating the spirit world from the material world became thinned, and visions and prophecies came through to those ready to receive them. Women, for whatever reason, seemed particularly receptive during the new moon. Magdalena knew the old wisdom was shunned among the new-thinking men, so that's why she didn't emphasize it. The practicality of night fishing during the full moon left the new moon available. Not all women bled at the new moon, but a good percentage did, and the three days of rest had an irresistible appeal to them, especially since Magdalena provided minders for the small children in a separate room.

Families of followers were scattered all along the western shore of the Sea of Galilee. A few lived in Magdala, so they arrived first at the house and helped Keturah and Zeno with whatever needed doing. Many lived six miles away in Capernaum where Yeshua had his house. His mother Mary had been living with him since her husband Joseph died. Some traveled all the way from Bethsaida at the top of the lake. Their journey could take an entire day, and they arrived dusty and tired. Some, like Mother Mary and any pregnant women, rode donkeys or mules, but most of them walked, carrying their bedrolls and food sacks on their heads. Those were festive, gossipy walks, as the women looked forward to being together with other women.

They also looked forward to Magdalena's lessons. She made the master's teaching come alive with practices they had never learned, and she taught practical arts like the making of healing oils and ointments, and the clever use of spices and herbs in cooking. The new bride Eunice also helped by teaching reading and writing Greek to those women who desired to learn. Most people didn't need to read, but Eunice and Magdalena knew that literacy empowered whoever had the skill, and the more women who had it the better. Going to Magdala for New Moon School was a highlight of the women's month.

"Oh, my goodness, Aliza. You look like you could give birth any minute," said Magdalena, helping a very bulky young woman down from her donkey. "I'm surprised Ben let you come."

"Well, I told him all the best midwives would be here, too, so I am in good hands if the baby comes."

Magdalena laughed. "Very true. Come in, and let me wash your feet. We will make you comfortable."

Some of the early arrivals had spread their beds in the courtyard and were resting in the quiet. Others sat against the walls in silent prayer, eyes closed and palms open. Magdalena had taught them the silent prayer she had learned from the master, and the women prayed at least three times per day. Except during the meals, stillness prevailed in the courtyard, unless a baby cried for the breast or an inconsolable toddler ran in from the nursery room. Many of the women said the quiet was their favorite part of the secluded time.

When the day was ending and fifteen women had arrived, Magdalena called them to sit in a circle around the courtyard.

"The master sometimes teaches that the first will be last and the last will be first. In a circle, there is no first or last. We are all the same. Also, in a circle, the power of God is intensified, as some of you have already experienced. That is why we sit in a circle. Now, please close your eyes, and I will guide you to imagine an encounter with God. We know that our imaginations are a gift from God, and God uses our imaginations to contact us, just as in dreams. If you open your mind to see and hear from the divine, God can be with you.

"Now imagine you are walking on a path near some water. The sun is warm, and there are trees nearby for shade. Coming towards you on the path is another person who emanates light. As the person approaches, you see that it is God, and God's arms are open, desiring to embrace you. Allow yourself to embrace God. Look into God's eyes. God says to you, 'Child, what do you want to know?' Let yourself ask a question and hear the answer. Now ask God what name God prefers you to use in addressing God. Hear the answer. God kisses you and blesses you, saying farewell for now and walking on the path, leaving you to happily return to this courtyard. Welcome back."

Some of the women immediately opened their eyes, bursting to tell of their visions. Others stayed silent with eyes closed. When all eyes were opened, the women told of their encounters with God. In the cacophony of speech, these phrases arose:

"My God is a woman. She is so kind."

"My God wants to be called Infinite Love. He looked like a man at first, but then shifted into a woman."

"My God is the Sculptor of the Universe. His arms were strong and muscular, and he held me tight."

"Mine is Ground of Being."

"She said she is I Am, and she pointed out that she never said she was male."

"My God is Eternal Light and has no gender at all. All I saw was light, but I felt loved."

"If so many of us see God as female or not-male, why do we always say 'he'?"

The talk continued along these lines during dinner. Zeno and Keturah opened the kitchen to the women, and they dined on bread, cheese, fish, fruits, and olives.

Oil lamps lit the evening session where, after silent prayer, Magdalena asked a question. "The master teaches that when we can make the inside like the outside and the outside like the inside, we will enter heaven. What do you think he means?"

After a long pause in which no one volunteered to answer, Mother Mary spoke. "Maybe he means that your inner heart and your outer actions are the same. You don't pretend to be someone or something you are not."

"Yes, I was thinking that," said Rhoda. "You don't put on airs."

"You tell the truth about what you are feeling, open-hearted like."

"Single-minded and single-hearted. Undivided."

Magdalena asked further, "And how close are you to being like that?" Silence. "Now, don't be ashamed. There is no shame here, among equals, among sisters. Tell us."

"I have so much anger in me, and I never let people know it. I am as sweet as honey on the outside, but my inside is raging."

"Mine is fear. We have been married two years, and no baby yet. I am afraid Aaron will divorce me any day, but I haven't told him or anyone how I feel. I just cry myself to sleep after he starts snoring." Around the room, others nodded their agreement.

"My dear sisters, close your eyes again, and go to that imagination place you were in before. Picture a scene of your anger, or your fear, or your shame, whatever it is you are hiding inside under an outside of sweetness. Now, take that anger, fear, or shame in your hands and roll it into a ball. Squeeze it tight. Now open your hand and let it float away into the sky. What do you see?" She paused to look at the women's faces. Some had creased brows, some had beatific smiles, some were releasing

31

sighs of pent up breath. "Now, open your eyes and tell us."

"I saw a hand come down from the sky and take the ball!"

"So did I!"

"And how do you feel now about your outside and your inside?"

"One step closer to making them the same."

"Relieved."

"I feel so much love for my God who would be willing to take that ball from me. She does love me."

"Thank you, Magdalena. You help me understand. May Infinite Love bless you."

The women arose, embraced, and wished each other good-night. Mothers collected their children to bed down with them. Some slept in the courtyard, open to the starry sky, while others spread out into the rooms of Magdalena's large house. What wonders would tomorrow's lessons reveal?

After breakfast and silent prayer, Magdalena asked the women to enter the place of vision they had entered the day before. "Today, we will visit the realm of God. Now the master says, 'kingdom of God' or 'kingdom of heaven,' but kingdom implies male, and many of us see God differently, so let's call it the realm of ---insert your God-name. The realm of I am. The realm of infinite love. The realm of eternal light." She paused and saw the women smile as they called the divine by the names they had been given. "Now picture yourself standing overlooking a town. It may be a new town or one you are familiar with. The master teaches that the realm of heaven is here now. You are looking down on the realm right now. That is it, below you there. I want you to observe it, noting all the details." She paused for the women to imagine, then she guided gently. "Observe the people, their actions and words... Observe the houses, barns, streets...Observe nature in and around the town..." Magdalena gave them a good long time to imagine. Meanwhile, Zeno put a short stick on the ground in front of each woman. "Now, when you open your eyes, I want you to write or draw in the sand in front of you something to help you remember your vision. It can be a list of words to describe what you saw or a sketch of the scene. Don't talk yet, just write or draw. Begin...now."

Those women who had no letters drew simple shapes. The writers made word lists or whole sentences. Artists composed complete scenes of their visions. A few women never picked up the sticks, just sat quietly, some with scowls on their faces. Magdalena heard a demon-voice start to say, "Look, you are failing with those women. They hate you," but she let it float up into the grasp of the unseen hand. What did the master always say?--- "those who have ears to hear." Not everyone among the male disciples had ears to hear, and the same would be true of the women. She couldn't reach everyone, but she was happy to see that every month more women responded than didn't.

"So, sisters, what did you see?"

"It was beautiful."

"Everyone was acting out of love."

"We were mixed in with the men in the synagogue."

"There were no beggars."

"The animals were big and healthy, the trees and vines, too."

"My husband asked me if I wanted sex, rather than just jumping on me."

"We all felt safe."

"Every house had a crowd around the table,

33

laughing."

"Each person's outside was the same as their inside." This answer, from Eunice, stopped the discussion, as it sank in that the realm of Infinite Love depended on the undivided hearts of the people. Very few people had undivided hearts, but it was not impossible for people to have them. The realm of heaven was nearer than they thought; it was "at hand" as the master often said, if only they could make the inside and the outside the same. Another of the master's teachings had come clear, thanks to Magdalena. The female followers no longer felt they were lagging behind the males in understanding. Perhaps they were even ahead.

Months passed and the tandem wisdom schools of Yeshua and Magdalena gained students. Yeshua tended to follow the promptings of his inner voice and round up men he saw fishing or carrying out their daily work. "Come, follow me," he would say, and they would follow. Magdalena stayed near her home in Magdala and waited for word of mouth to bring the women to her. Some with ears to hear had become staunch members of the school, never missing a month unless there was a birth, death, or other emergency. Every month, they brought new students to sit in Magdalena's circle. Some left and never returned after seeing the strange practices Magdalena taught. Perhaps they decided to rely on their men to interpret the master's words to them. She had a niggling sense that some of them were gossiping around the community, giving her a bad reputation, but she handed that worry to the invisible hand.

She was sure that part of the gossip had to do

with her relationship with the master. Traditionally, betrothed couples lived apart for as long as a year before finalizing their contract by consummating the marriage and living together. Magdalena's situation as a widow was different, and her soul partnership with Yeshua was more than a betrothal, more than a marriage even. They often shared a bed at her home or at his, and they walked hand in hand, kissing each other on the lips when they felt like it. No wonder people in and out of the community of believers started calling her names. Let them talk. She and Yeshua knew that their contract had not been consummated; they slept in each other's arms for comfort and affection. As their love grew, they talked of lovemaking, but Yeshua said he was waiting for a sign that it was time. Both of them waited patiently, and Magdalena considered herself highly favored.

One day, a messenger arrived with an invitation from Yeshua's mother, Mary, asking her to come and stay for several days. Mary attended the New Moon School regularly and was one of those who had ears to hear. Magdalena appreciated it when Mary gave her wise and loving interpretations of scripture. Happily, she sent the messenger back with a 'yes' and called Zeno to start packing. As gifts, she took a large jar of pickled fish, a coffer of assorted spices, and a liniment of frankincense and juniper good for aches in the limbs. She had noticed that Mary sometimes had difficulty arising from the floor of the courtyard after sitting long in prayer.

Mary herself greeted her and Zeno as they led Sophia up to the Capernaum house.

"Welcome, Daughter! Welcome, Zeno. Come in and bathe your feet after that dusty walk. The master is talking to some of the followers in the courtyard. He asked especially for you to join them, Zeno. He says you have ears to hear."

Zeno smiled and bowed his head to her as he joined the men in the courtyard. Mary ushered Magdalena into the kitchen.

"Yeshua is sometimes frustrated with his students. He says they lack imagination. I told him to send them to your school. Imagination is our favorite thing there, along with silence. Magdalena, I also want to speak to you about something disturbing I heard. One of those women who stopped attending is Peter's wife. She has been filling his ears with evil ideas about you, and I think he needs watching. He could be an enemy in the making."

"Peter? He is one of Yeshua's favorites. They love each other."

"Perhaps, but keep your eyes open. It is so easy for men to destroy a woman's reputation. I was on the verge of ruin myself when I conceived Yeshua; if I Am hadn't sent angels to rescue me, I would not be here. You are precious to me, my son, and the women followers. You must be careful."

"Yes, I will. Thank you, dear Mother." And Magdalena kissed Mary's cheek.

That evening, as the sun faded, Yeshua took Magdalena by the hand and said, "Let's pray." He led her up the hill behind the house to an old, gnarled olive tree whose trunk was corrugated into separate grooves. "This is my favorite prayer tree," he said. "My back fits perfectly into one of the grooves, and I can sit here for hours just listening for God's voice. Which groove do you want?"

"I will take this one on the opposite side," Magdalena said, and sat with her back cradled in the trunk. The oily smell of the olives smashed on the ground made her feel anointed, holy. No wonder her love liked praying here.

Peter, Levi, and Judas watched the two stealing away, hand in hand.

"Now, where do you suppose they are going?" asked Peter. "For a little tussle in the bushes? Let's go see. Maybe we'll catch them in the act." And he led the two others in pursuit.

When they found the lovers in silent prayer, leaning chastely against a tree, Peter snorted.

"Well, how sweet. Not what I would expect of that whore."

"Peter! Don't call her that," said Levi. "She is much beloved of the master and the women."

"The women! We don't need the women. This is a men's movement. I tell you, the master is the messiah, and as such, we need to be prepared to fight alongside him. Women are too weak to fight. They will just hold us back. I don't like that whore teaching our women a bunch of witchcraft and such."

"She is only teaching the master's words in a way women can understand, not witchcraft."

"Are you sure? My wife gave me an earful of what the whore is up to, and it looks dubious to me. Let's go back to the house."

"I'll be there in a minute," said Levi. He observed the two under the olive tree for several minutes, and they didn't move their lips or their bodies. He thought he saw a greenish glow under the shadow of the tree. Rubbing his eyes, he went back to the house. He would ask Yeshua about the prayer.

———————••———————

"Yes, Levi, I taught the silent prayer to the male

followers once before you joined us, but they were not ready for it. They squirmed, laughed, and complained. If you are interested, join Mary and me any time. We will be glad for your company. More hearts together make for a powerful prayer."

"Please," Levi said, smiling. "I would like to learn."

"We will be under the olive tree at dawn tomorrow." And the master put his hand on Levi's shoulder as encouragement. "Now, let's eat with the others."

Peter, Judas, Andrew, and several other male followers were reclining in the courtyard of the house the master had built, eating the meal Mary provided. Levi took a seat across the space to be near the master. Magdalena sat with Mary just inside the kitchen where they could hear the discussion but not intrude on the men's dinner.

Andrew had a question. "Master, don't you think we should confine our healing and preaching to men only? Women have much work to do in the home, and we shouldn't take them away from the place they shine."

"Do you think the shape of woman's body makes her different in her heart?"

"Yes! They are loving of children and care about flowers and pretty things that we have no time for. I think they are very different."

"I think their concern for unimportant things makes them unfit to fight against the Romans and too limited to learn from you," Peter said.

Magdalena caught Mary's eye but said nothing.

The master shook his head. "Women are made in the image of God just like men are. That means God approves of women as much as men. They can learn and teach and see visions as well as men can, or sometimes better. Gender is an illusion attached only to the body.

It has no meaning in the realm of love. The sooner you let go of your ideas about males being better, the sooner you will enter the realm."

Peter cast an angry look across to the kitchen where Magdalena's hem was visible in the doorway. "And my wife tells me that the women's school is teaching how to make potions to prevent children and put husbands to sleep. Why must they meet in the dark of the moon like witches?"

"Peter, you are angry for no reason. Let go of your rage and let the women be. I think we should go to bed. Tomorrow, we are going over the sea to visit Bethsaida. We all need rest." The master's departure ended the meeting.

Yeshua and Magdalena slept in one of the rooms off of the courtyard. In the hours before dawn, she had a nightmare vision in which she was walking by the sea with a long line of her women learners. They carried their sandals in their hands and splashed in the small waves that lapped the shore. Suddenly, a shadow fell across their path, and a large bird with something in its beak flew directly over her head. A sharp rock fell from the bird's grip directly onto Magdalena's head, knocking her into darkness. A hole opened in the sand and she slipped down into a dark tunnel. When the tunnel became light, she was standing on a stone-paved street in a city she had never seen. She was the only woman in the crowd of hundreds of men watching a parade coming down the street. The marching men wore long robes, some black, some purple, some red. Some had pointed hats on their heads, but all were carrying gold crosses on tall poles. There were thousands of them; their line stretched as far as she could see. Their heads were high and their shoulders powerful. Where were they going?

She looked and saw the vanguard of the column climbing the steps of a huge domed building of white marble. She knew only men were admitted there and that her vision was a true scene of the future. When she woke there were tears in her eyes.

"Mary, my love. What did you dream?"

"As much as you try to convince Peter and the men that women are worthy, the men will win."

"Do you want to give up?"

"No. That was only one vision of one time. Not enough to make me lose hope. I will stick by you, my husband."

"My Mary. My tower of strength." And Yeshua kissed his beloved good-morning. "We have morning prayer with Levi. He wants to learn."

"See? There is hope."

Levi joined them beneath the olive tree, and Magdalena felt a new energy swirling about the three of them as they sat silently. It seemed to arise from the roots of the tree like a fountain, lifting their prayers up through the branches to heaven. Levi's presence added to their strength, and her love reached out to him as an ally. When they stood together afterwards, she saw a new light in Levi's eyes.

"I feel so at peace," he said.

She smiled.

"Let's eat some breakfast and hurry down to the boats," the master said.

Magdalena hated boats. Often, her most frightening visions featured water crossings in leaky or rudderless boats. She said, "Yeshua, I will not join you today. I told Zeno that I would choose what items I want him to take to Sepphoris to sell in the market, so I will return to my house. Besides, the next New Moon School is in a few

40

days."

"You just don't like boats."

Magdalena laughed. "True. But those other things are true, too." Yeshua kissed her.

"Let me escort you home to Magdala," Levi offered. "I can help Zeno at the market, too. I am a tenacious haggler."

"I can tell you never were a fisherman, Levi. You hate boats, too," the master said. Levi just smiled, and the three returned to Mother Mary's house to eat with the other followers.

Later, as Magdalena and Levi walked alongside Sophia on the road to Magdala, they spoke of the silent prayer and how it affected him. Levi also asked why she was selling things in the market.

"The master has talked to me about not clinging to things of this world. He says that the fewer goods I own, the lighter will be my spirit, and the freer I will be. Besides, the extra money I can give to the followers for their needs: travel, food, lodging. A few of the other women also have their own means, and we all want to give as much as we can. There's a big trip to Jerusalem coming up at Passover, and that will cost a good deal."

Levi looked stricken. "Has the master told you what is to happen on that trip?"

"No. Celebrating the Passover with all the other pilgrims, I expect."

"He has told some of us that he is going to be betrayed and killed on that trip. Many of us didn't pay him any mind. We acted as if he was joking, but there was a look in his eyes. I think he meant it."

Magdalena's heart sank. Yeshua didn't joke about things like that. "It wasn't one of his cryptic parables, was it?"

41

Levi looked straight into her face and shook his head.

"Well," she said, keeping her voice level, "I will ask him about it when I see him next. I will ask him to explain it in plain terms, so women can understand it."

"Now you are the one joking," Levi said. "The master has told me many times that the women grasp his teachings much faster than we men. Why do you think that is?"

"He teaches us to love and let go of power and control. Women are better at surrendering than men, maybe because we have so little power to start with. And you don't have to tell most of us to love, especially where children, the sick, and the weak are concerned. We do it naturally. Some of us think his whole teaching is tailored to women. That's why we love him so."

Levi nodded. Zeno had seen them approaching and came out to meet them, taking Sophia's lead and welcoming them heartily.

"Levi! What a surprise."

"I'm coming to market with you. Nobody haggles better than I do. We will get the best prices for Magdalena's trinkets. After all, it's for a good cause."

"Indeed. Come in and rest. I have food prepared."

Magdalena smiled at Zeno. Like Levi, he was one of the open-hearted men who understood what the master meant. Yeshua had often praised Zeno to her. She wished all the male followers were like him. But then she remembered that Zeno was not a normal man but a eunuch. Like a woman, he was considered a lesser person, unworthy of power. Did one have to be an outcast to appreciate what the master said?

After supper, Magdalena started handing items to Zeno and Levi who put them in sacks and packs for transport to the market in Sepphoris. Down came the

decorative lamps from the wall and the copper cups
Tiras had brought home from one of his journeys. The
jeweled candle sticks could go, along with the tapestry
he had brought from Egypt. Utilitarian pots and dishes
she kept, for there was always the need for large
meals at the school. The same was true of carpets and
cushions. Finally, she brought out her jewel box and gave
the whole thing to Zeno.

"My lady, don't you want to keep one or two
ornaments to wear?"

"They are just things, dear one. And they will fetch
good money, especially this gold necklace. Don't let them
cheat you on that one. It's real gold. These bangles and
hair clips are only bronze, but some have good stones
in them. Oh, and the pearls are worth a lot." Magdalena
paused then removed an amethyst ring from her finger.
Jubal had given her that. She had only started wearing it
when Tiras died; before that she kept it hidden. But what
did she need with an old lover's ring, now that she was
betrothed to Yeshua? She handed it to Zeno and looked
away.

"There, I feel lighter already," she said. "Early bed,
I think. You gentlemen have a long day ahead of you
tomorrow. Good night." And she retired to her room.

Tears poured from her eyes when she was alone,
and she was not sure they were from taking off Jubal's
ring or the ominous remark Levi had made about the
Jerusalem trip. Why had Yeshua told the men and not
her? Not wanting to cause her fear, of course. She and
her beloved weren't even fully married yet, and she
was facing losing him. How could this possibly be God's
plan? How could it lead them to the realm? She took
deep breaths, trying to let the worry go. Eventually, she
slept. The dream vision that came in the early morning

hours was of Judas. First, she saw Judas smiling at all the disciples, seated around a table. He went from one to the other, kissing each on the cheek, including herself. Last, he kissed Yeshua on the lips and the scene changed to a solitary tree on a dark hill. From a distance, she could see something hanging there, but she couldn't make out what it was. A body? She awoke with a start. The message was true, she knew, but incomplete.

Chapter 5

Tabor

When the master and disciples returned from across the sea and the New Moon School had finished its three days, Yeshua asked Magdalena to prepare for a trip to Mt. Tabor.

"What for?"

"A wedding."

"Whose?"

He smiled, and she leapt into his arms.

"Yes, I will start immediately. Can Zeno and Levi come? They should be home from Sepphoris in a day or so."

"No, but I will ask some others to accompany us."

She didn't argue or ask for details. In her heart, she yearned to secure her beloved for herself as soon as possible.

When Magdalena set foot on the trail to ascend Mt. Tabor, the drizzle began. The usually dusty plants along the trail perked up, and the stones took on a colorful sheen. Of course the land needed the rain, but her hair and clothes were growing limp and soggy. She looked at Yeshua.

"And why did you choose this day to climb the mountain?"

He smiled and answered, "I just knew this was the day for us to wed. Trust me."

She laughed. "I trust you, but our witnesses don't look too happy." They glanced back over their shoulders to see Peter, Andrew, and John struggling up the slope, slipping on the muddy layer atop the sand, and muttering. "I wish we could have brought Zeno and Levi."

"Yes, but this will work out. Don't you feel Love's blessing upon you?"

"Well, I'm having no trouble climbing, unlike those fellows. I'm not even winded."

"A sure sign that you are on the right path."

When they reached the mountain top, they turned and waited for the others. The drizzle had stopped, and the sun wanted to peek through the clouds. Magdalena felt a shiver in her bones. Something was going to happen, greater than just a wedding.

As the group assembled in a loose circle, the clouds parted and a ray of sun struck the ground. Suddenly, there stood three figures, with green light emanating from their heads. Magdalena's eyes widened in awe. She knew them to be Moses, the prophet Elijah, and Holy Wisdom, the female spirit who had helped create the universe. Wisdom, dressed all in white with white hair, beckoned the lovers to approach. Magdalena expected Wisdom to have a wrinkled, aged face to match her white hair, but her face was beautiful and young. She

smiled kindly at Magdalena. The three holy figures
joined hands around the betrothed, bowed their heads,
and prayed a blessing silently. No one heard any words,
but the ears of her heart felt the message. Her marriage
to Yeshua had divine support, in spite of what human
law and custom might say.

Then a voice spoke from the sky between the broken
clouds. It might have been the same voice she heard
by the Jordan, but it sounded like a woman's voice,
then it didn't. It said, "These are my beloved children.
They are one. Listen to them. Both of them." A bright
ribbon of all the rainbow colors swooped down upon
the mountain and encircled Magdalena and Yeshua. The
holy figures disappeared, and the bride and groom were
wrapped round and round in the rainbow ribbon. In the
rainbow's energy, she felt herself beginning to melt into
her beloved. She was losing her edges as she overflowed
into him and he into her. Her logical mind had to ask if
this were a dream or reality, and the vision snapped. She
was standing on a muddy mountain top in her husband's
arms, and three skeptics looked on from a distance.

"We can't report this," Peter whispered to his
companions.

"We have to," John said, shocked that Peter would
suggest lying about something so holy and important.

"Don't you see? If we want to keep the women out,
we can't tell them Holy Wisdom was here and God said
to listen to them both."

Andrew asked, "But what can we do?"

"We'll think of something," Peter hissed.

The disciples embraced the bride and groom with
more or less enthusiasm, and the party descended
the mountain. At Magdala, the disciples continued
on to Capernaum, leaving the newlyweds to sleep at

Magdalena's house. Zeno had come home in her absence and had set the large purse of money he had received in exchange for her "trinkets" on the kitchen table. He had also prepared a meal, complete with wine from Tiras's cellar.

"Welcome home, my lady, my lord. Is it true that your wedding was attended by Moses and Elijah?"

"Yes, Zeno. We are now truly married by heaven. And hungry to match!" Yeshua laughed.

"Come eat, come eat! And wine to celebrate!"

The couple ate in a silence of bliss, enjoying the bridal foods that boded good luck and many children. After dark, they looked into each other's eyes, and a new light shone between them. Magdalena knew the look a man's eyes take on when he is yearning for physical love. She had seen it at its most carnal in Tiras and at its most passionate in Jubal. She had never seen it in Yeshua's eyes, until now. He had always given her brotherly looks, like a comrade. Now he looked at her with a lover's hunger. She smiled archly and returned the look as a woman does when she feels the thrill of seduction stir within. They rose together and went to their marriage bed, Yeshua leading her by the fingertips of her hand. She floated behind him.

With Tiras, Magdalena had felt used. He had spent his lust on her body roughly and abruptly, caring not at all whether she enjoyed his attentions. It was a nightly chore she endured, unless she could slip something into his wine to put him to sleep before he approached her. With Jubal, their illicit passion was stealthy. When they came to the act, their climaxes were both explosive and brief. She enjoyed the sensation of being desired by someone other than her husband, but their affair was short-lived. Nothing had prepared her for making love to

Yeshua.

Magdalena knew that the master called the body God's temple, but no one had ever touched her as if she were a temple until that night. Yeshua undressed her and ran his hands reverently over her shoulders, arms, breasts, stomach, and thighs. His hands read her, inch by inch, and she shivered with pleasure she had never known. She reached out to read his body, and he allowed it, closing his eyes at the intimacy and honesty of it. When every part was known to the hand, Yeshua kissed every inch of her. She had never been so honored and loved. Perhaps her mother had adored her infant body like this, but she had no memory of it. When they lay down together, Magdalena sensed a shift in the atmosphere of the room. A verdant light came through the window and drew an oblong on the floor from which arose the scent of cinnamon and clove. Slowly, ever slowly, Yeshua wrapped his being around hers and she began to melt into him as she had on the mountain. She flowed and waved in a liquid state, surrendering to his movements. The waves started small, little ripples on the foreshore, then grew and swelled to a rhythmic dance. Soon the swells lifted her up and up, then she subsided on the other side of the wave. Then up and up again, raised by a power she could only succumb to. Though she feared the power of the sea, she let go of all fear in his arms and let herself be lifted, dropped, lifted, and lifted higher. Behind her eyes a rainbow burst into light, all the colors swirling into and around the others, all one, all united. At that moment, she felt the most luscious pleasure she had ever felt. She wanted it to last forever, never to fade or fall. And she knew that this was the realm of infinite love. She had only glimpsed it before in visions, but now she felt it. Yeshua had taken her there. This was the bridal chamber, and the *Song of Songs* suddenly made sense.

"Oh, can we stay?" she breathed.

"Not now," he whispered. "But we can return." When they slept, each had gained from their union. She had glimpsed the realm of infinite love, and he had worshiped the flesh of woman. Neither would be the same.

Peter grumbled as he walked along with Andrew, heading for the lake shore.

"What is happening to him? Ever since he married that witch, he has been talking to women. Either he seeks them out, or they are drawn to him somehow. That slut by the well, that bleeding woman, that naked whore they pulled straight out of bed where she was screwing her paramour. And how does he treat them? Like they matter. Like they are worth his time."

Andrew said, "He has always been kind to women."

"Not so! Remember that hag in Sidon? He called her a bitch and told her the kingdom is not for her. That's the way to deal with pagan women---any women if you ask me."

"Yes, but he healed her daughter anyway."

"And after that trip up Tabor, he has become a ladies' healer. It sticks in my craw."

"Calm down, Peter. We can keep control of things, even if we let the women in a little."

"Well, just remember to stick to the story: Moses and Elijah *only* were up on that hill, and it had nothing to do with a wedding. The voice said 'Listen to him,' not them, and Yeshua got all sparkly, and that was it. If she says different, it's a woman's word against three men."

"Right. Got it. And Judas is with us, too. He won't say anything."

"From here on out, we will have to keep an eye on her. We can twist anything she does to our advantage. Yeshua loves us best."

"I'm not sure about that, Peter," Andrew said. "He loves her a lot."

Peter scoffed, and the two kept walking.

———————— • ————————

At the next session of New Moon School, Magdalena wanted to talk about marital issues, so she asked only married or betrothed women to attend. Of course, this piqued the interest of widows and virgins, and she had a full courtyard when the women arrived.

"Sisters, I must warn you that I will be teaching openly about some ideas unknown to the unmarried girls among us, and I don't want you to be shocked or embarrassed. If you want to leave now, I understand, but I am going to be honest."

Rhoda, one of the virgins, spoke up. "Sister Magdalena, I trust you to tell me things that will improve my life and my knowledge of the divine. I promise not to blush." Other women nodded their assent.

"Fine. After supper we will begin with a scripture and a vision."

The women took their places on the ground and along the walls. Zeno had brought a wicker stool from the market in Sepphoris for Mother Mary, and she sat comfortably on it. Magdalena guided them to a vision of Eden and asked them to watch Adam and Eve's interaction. Then she transported the women to a luxurious, dark bedchamber and asked them to imagine details of the scene that she selected from *Song of Songs*. Then, she read to them from that most bridal of scriptures and let them form pictures in their minds.

Afterwards, some women had blissful smiles, some were half asleep, and others looked ashamed. Magdalena said, "Tell me what you saw and felt, in Eden or in the chamber." The women were shy to start. Finally, Rhoda said,

"I saw God's hand with a knife, cutting Adam open and taking out his rib. He was screaming and thrashing on the ground. He had been perfectly whole and fine before, but now he was wounded and diminished. It was horrible."

"I saw Adam and Eve sleeping innocently in each other's arms in the beautiful garden. All was perfect. They didn't even need any blankets. They were friends, but I felt it wouldn't last."

"I'm embarrassed to say that I felt pleasure in the chamber. I wanted to stay there longer."

Magdalena smiled. "The lovemaking was good there?"

"Yes, much better than reality, I'm sorry to say." Some of the women laughed in sympathy.

"Would it surprise you if I told you that one of the paths to the realm of infinite love is through the marriage bed? I see some of you nodding. Let's talk about what lovemaking is like for you and your husband. And how it is different from the scripture's description in the *Song*. Unmarried women, pay attention here. You may need this later." The women laughed.

"Quick."

"Painful."

"Routine"

"Rough"

"Chore"

"I get pregnant all the time."

"Wonderful." The women looked at Eunice who had spoken.

"Tell us more, Eunice."

"Well, we don't have a rich chamber with spices and exotic fruits, but Jude treats me with gentleness and patience. He is slow, beginning with a lot of kisses and touches. Then, when he is in me, he moves slowly and makes it last as long as he can. I almost always enjoy it very much."

"Do you ever feel that you are doing something holy or divine?"

"Yes, sometimes."

"Sisters, God is love, and that includes love between men and women. Don't think it's just all abstract and ethereal. We are made in God's image, and our two images can unite in a way that makes us even more like God."

One of the women took in her breath at that, scandalized. "You are talking about ritual sex like the pagans practice. Shame on you!"

"No, I am talking about healing the breach between men and women and God. Adam was whole until his rib was ripped out, you said. Now he is diminished. If male and female could unite, we could be whole humans. One way to unite is in lovemaking. Another is in mutual respect. Another is in making gender not matter. The master teaches that."

Magdalena could sense that some of the women were disturbed by her teaching. She had pushed the women far along the path, and it was too much for some of them. She foresaw that there would be gossip and more calling of names after this meeting. But this new revelation she had discovered in the arms of Yeshua was too important to keep to herself. Why shouldn't all women have the same bliss she had? After that, she taught about ointments to ease the pain for those women who saw relations as a hurtful chore. She taught about laserwort tea for those women who were afraid of another pregnancy. She talked about patience on the part of man and woman. When the women departed on the third day, Magdalena felt drained and a little afraid. Maybe, like the male disciples, the female followers lacked ears to hear.

Eunice had hung back. "Magdalena, thanks for that lesson. Women gripe so much about having sex with their husbands, I thought I was abnormal to enjoy it. I am glad you think it is good, and a way to God. Do you think men and women will ever respect and honor each other, except in the marriage bed?"

"The master says so. That is the realm he preaches, a place where gender dissolves and we are all just human, loving and helping each other. When it will come, I don't know, but we have to keep hoping."

"Yes. I can't wait to tell Jude about what I learned!" and she kissed Magdalena on the cheek and left.

Magdalena needed to be with Yeshua, so she called Zeno to bring Sophia so she could ride up to Capernaum to stay the night there.

In bed that night, after joining her husband and God as one, she dared to broach the subject on her mind and heart. "Beloved, are you really going to die in Jerusalem?"

"Who told you that?"

"Levi."

He took her in his arms and held her secure.

"Mary, love is stronger than death. I have said that often, and now we will prove it. Love never breaks, no matter how it is stretched across miles or millennia. Our love, especially, can withstand any separation because it depends less on our seeing and touching than some other loves. Ours is forged in true humanity and true spirit."

Magdalena's eyes filled with tears and she buried her sobs in his chest. "But I *want* to see you, and I *want* to touch you."

"Yes. You still cling to those elements of love, but do you see that the love itself doesn't depend on those?"

"I don't know what I see. I know I will lose you, and I just found you."

"You will never lose me, only my physical body. A visionary like you can always see me and speak to me, no matter where I am. I am with you beyond the current times."

"But why must you die? What is God thinking?"

Yeshua smiled. "That question will live on till the world ends. You are only the first to ask it. Even I cannot answer it. I just know it is right."

"Are you afraid?"

"Yes, for the pain in my body. And for the pain you and the others will suffer."

"Oh, my love, I will stay by you. I promise."

"You will be one of very few."

"What do you mean?"

"Have you not had a vision of my betrayal?"

"Yes, I have had two that I am aware of, but I don't know what they mean. I saw Judas kissing you and then I saw a body hanging from a tree."

"Judas has his role in all of this."

"To betray you?"

"And what was the other vision?"

She hesitated to tell him. Peter was his favorite

after her. "It was Peter. You always call him your rock. He knocked me unconscious with a rock and I saw the future of your followers. They excluded all women."

Yeshua sighed.

She added, "But I am only a human seer. My visions may not be right. Perhaps none of this will come to pass."

"No, my beloved, God speaks through you. But don't be afraid. It will come right in the end."

"But when?"

"You always ask the hard questions. I don't know. That depends on humans and how they grow. It will take a while in human years, but to God it already is. That's why little things like touching and dying don't matter. It will come right."

"What happens when we die?"

"We all return to God's love. We are made of God's love, and that love lives within us and all around us. Nothing is ever destroyed. It just returns to its primal form and rejoins God. So there is nothing to fear."

She shook her head. "This is too much for me, husband. Just hold me." And the two slept in their bed of love and heartbreak.

Before dawn, a vision comforted her. She and Yeshua stood atop a mountain. He carried a large jar of wine. She carried one of water. In front of them stood a stone bowl. They poured the contents of their jars into the bowl until it overflowed. The wine and water never ran out, and a trickle flowed down the mountainside. It grew into a river then a torrent. They stopped pouring but the torrent still flowed. Yeshua kissed her then leapt into the river, sliding away from her down the mountain. She kept her eye on him until he disappeared in the current. She cried out, "My love!" and dipped her hand into the bowl. When she touched the wine, she could feel her beloved's presence. She could hear his voice saying "I am with you. Don't be afraid." When she raised her eyes to the horizon, she saw a glowing white figure walking away from her. With her hand still in the wine, she heard, "I am with you." When she woke, Yeshua smiled into her face. He had been watching her dream.

"Another good one?" he asked.

Laughing, she took her beloved into her arms. She would stick by his side from now on. No more letting him roam around Galilee with the men, healing and teaching. She wanted as many of those unimportant touches and kisses as she could receive in the time she had left.

Chapter 6

Jerusalem

The seventy miles from Galilee to Jerusalem would take the party at least a week to traverse. Yeshua expected to teach in the villages along the way, staying with hosts that offered or camping by the roadside. Traveling south through Samaria was dangerous, so scouts went ahead to reconnoiter. Magdalena asked Zeno to hitch Sophia to the donkey cart and loaded the cart with necessities: water jugs, dried and preserved foods, bedding and tents, lamps and pots, herbs and medicines. Excitement battled with fear in her heart. The journey would be an adventure, but the destination loomed dark.

Just before the caravan crossed from Galilee into Samaria, a group of ten lepers appeared at a distance, on a rise. They called out to Yeshua to heal them, keeping away as lepers were expected to do. He declared them healed, and one of them came near to thank him. He was a Samaritan.

"I see only the Samaritan bothered to thank you," Magdalena said to her husband, walking by his side. "Not surprising."

"Why do you say that?"

"Gratitude comes easy to those who have little. Outcasts, slaves, women. The rich and powerful feel entitled to be served. At least that has been my experience."

"And those outcasts are closer to the realm than the rich. The rich are enjoying rewards here and now. That's all they'll get. Too bad they can't see it."

"But you teach them that all the time, my love."

"Yes, but they have no---"

"Ears to hear," she completed his usual sentence. He smiled into the face of his beloved wife.

After a couple of nights camping, the party entered a large town with a synagogue. Yeshua went to pray and teach there, since it was the sabbath. A crippled woman who could barely stand came to pray. Magdalena saw immediately that the master would have a dilemma to face: should he heal the woman and violate the sabbath law against work? How could he leave the woman to suffer longer? Magdalena knew what Yeshua would choose, and she tried not to fear the consequences. Just then, Yeshua was talking to a rich Pharisee, wearing fine sabbath robes. They smiled at each other, nodding as if they had made some kind of contract. Magdalena thought she saw dinner and lodging in the offing. After the readings, the teaching, and the prayers, the crippled woman approached the master. Without hesitation, he declared that her faith had healed her, and she stood up straight. The woman rejoiced, but some of the bystanders were scandalized. Magdalena suspected it would be an awkward dinner at the Pharisee's house, if they were admitted at all. Of course, only the men sat around the main room, the women being relegated to the kitchen and back pantry. She would have to hear about what Yeshua said and taught second-hand.

When he joined her in bed, he looked worn out.

"That was some dinner. Maybe we should have camped out another night," he said.

"Why? What did they attack you with?"

"Healing on the sabbath was the big one, but they also threw in my proclivity to associate with sinners and tax collectors, and my tendency to slack off on washing my hands for meals."

"No! They weren't rude enough to mention that!"

"Oh, yes. I talked about the inside and the outside and where the real dirt comes from."

Tears came into Magdalena's eyes. Yeshua noticed and put his arm around her.

"Don't worry."

"I just feel the hatred against you building up. The more you break their rules, the more they are going to want to destroy you."

"And you know in your heart it has to be that way."

"But I can't help wanting to save you, somehow."

He kissed the top of her head and whispered. "Love will win. I promise you."

She wanted to believe him, but she struggled against the coming pain.

Along the road south, more and more people joined the master's entourage. Their small family group had become a long, straggling train of followers. Just on the outskirts of Jericho, a blind beggar called to Yeshua from the side of the road, and the master healed him. Then the procession continued through the town. So many people lined the streets that they crushed each other.

People climbed on rooftops and tree branches to catch a glimpse of the great healer above the crowd. Suddenly, Yeshua called out to a man sitting in a tree.

"Hey, Zach! I see you up there. Aren't we all dining at your place today? Come on down and lead us to your house."

Startled, the little man nearly fell from the sycamore he had climbed and nervously joined the parade, leading the way to his commodious house. Magdalena had dropped behind Yeshua and was walking with Zeno and Levi, leading the donkey cart.

Levi laughed, "Say, I know that fellow! That's Zacchaeus. He's a tax collector like me. A rich one, though, and you know what that means. This should be interesting! At least the food will be plentiful." Magdalena let out a sigh. Another undesirable to besmirch her husband's reputation. She felt she was part of a landslide that was taking her down a hill she didn't want to descend, and there was nothing she could do to stop it.

Zach, however, turned out to be a generous host and a repentant crook. He made restitution to those he had cheated and became one of the followers. He and Levi used to have long talks about the tax business, one of the two-edged benefits Rome bestowed on the lands they colonized. The *Pax Romana* didn't come cheap.

When the caravan of followers arrived at Bethany, Mary and Martha greeted them in front of their brother Lazarus' house. Both smiled: Martha warmly and Mary with a bounce of excitement in her eyes. There was no doubt which was the elder sister. Martha wiped her hands on a towel from the kitchen and called out a hospitable greeting. Mary had eyes only for Yeshua. She hurried to his side, hoping for an embrace, which she received. They had been friends for years, and the raising of her brother from death had made Yeshua the family's hero. Magdalena saw the infatuation in Mary's adolescent eyes and smiled at it. Let her love the master. None of them would have him in arm's reach much longer.

Martha took Magdalena in her arms for a firm hug. "Oh, my sister, how I have longed to meet you since I heard of your betrothal to Yeshua. Come in, and let me bring you water and something to eat." Immediately, Magdalena felt at home and loved. Martha's soul spoke directly to hers, and they were firm friends in an instant.

Foot bowls cooled and cleansed the tired feet of the travelers, including the twelve, their wives, the widows, a few children, and servants. Mary personally washed Yeshua's feet and stuck by his side like a puppy.

"This is my brother Lazarus," Martha said, introducing Magdalena. "Brother, this is Magdalena, Yeshua's bride and one of the teachers."

"Welcome," he said, and subsided into silence. During their visit, Magdalena heard him speak no more than a dozen words. Later, she would ask Martha about him.

After welcomes and foot bathing, the company reclined or sat around the master to hear him teach. Urgent to convey his wisdom about life and the realm before it was too late, Yeshua spent every minute teaching when they were not walking, eating or sleeping. Young Mary sat at his feet, looking up into his eyes, rapt. She rested her hand near his foot, not daring to touch him but longing to.

Martha approached her sister and whispered sharply in her ear, "Mary, come help us in the kitchen."

Magdalena felt for both sisters. Putting her hand on Martha's arm, she said, "Never mind. I will help you," and steered the elder sister out of the room. Yeshua was about to rebuke Martha for trying to take Mary away, but Magdalena had forestalled the conflict. Mary settled back to soak up the master, his words, his looks, his being.

"That girl. I have no control of her. She goes her own way. Look at her, throwing herself at him. Shameful. And the rest of us with all these people to feed."

"We don't mind helping," said Eunice, who had already started unpacking the food she had brought to share. "We have heard Yeshua preach every day. We can stand to miss one lesson."

"And our brother Lazarus is useless. He never says a word to her about her behavior," Martha said.

"Lazarus seems very quiet. Has he always been that way?" Magdalena asked.

"No, he used to be quite boisterous. After he tasted death, he changed. He has that faraway look in his eyes and says little to us. It's like he has a secret he has to keep."

"Have you asked him about what he saw or experienced?"

"We tried. He just smiled, patted our hands, and said, 'It will be fine.' That's it. I am at my wit's end with those two."

Magdalena took Martha's hand. "Just let it be, my sister. It's not your job to fix either one of them. You can't control them. You can only love them."

Martha smiled. "I know that is true, but I torment myself. I am so glad you are here to speak this wisdom to me." She embraced Magdalena again, even though she had a drippy half-pomegranate in her hand. Eunice and Rhoda looked on, smiling. They, too had often received Magdalena's healing advice, especially where family problems were concerned.

"I noticed the rough skin on Lazarus's arms. Does it bother him?"

"That is left over from the tomb. He doesn't complain, but I have seen him rubbing it sometimes."

Magdalena bustled out the door, in the direction of the pack animals. "I have a salve that might help him." She returned with a box of oils, ointments, and medicines she always took along when she traveled. You never knew when someone would be bitten by a scorpion or get too much sun. "May I apply it to his scabs?"

"Of course," Martha said.

Magdalena held up the jar of ointment to Lazarus with a question in her smiling eyes. Lazarus nodded. No words were spoken as she gently spread the salve on his arms and lower legs, smoothing it into his skin. Lazarus closed his eyes and submitted to her attentions meekly. When she finished, his eyes met hers and a strong current of energy flowed between them. She saw the wise depths of his knowledge, and it calmed her soul. This man knew death first hand and was totally at peace. Nothing disturbed him. He had let go of the world and knew that it didn't matter. Only love remained in him, and she drank deeply from his eyes. Smiling, she arose and returned to the kitchen. In the door stood Martha, Eunice, and Rhoda. They had watched the whole scene, enthralled.

"Did he say anything?" Martha asked.

"Not with words," Magdalena said. Returning to her medicine box, she took out a small bottle. Gracefully, she crept into the main room where the master was speaking and knelt down beside Mary. She put the vial into the girl's hand and gestured that she could anoint the master's tired feet with it. Mary looked astonished then smiled. Magdalena watched from the kitchen door as Mary reverently and blissfully rubbed the rosemary scented oil onto his feet, heels and ankles. An aura of green light appeared around the young woman's head and she was beatified in Magdalena's eyes.

"You are a very trusting wife," Martha said. "I can't imagine most wives doing that."

"Fear wastes so much of our lives. It stops love from flowing out of us and into us. We have no time to waste on fear, my dear sister. If we have something to give, we must give it."

Martha's eyes brightened at this. Unexpectedly, she asked Magdalena, "Do you think I should marry?"

All three Galilean women laughed.

"Yes. You have so much love to give to a husband and children."

"I have felt tied to my brother, like it was my duty to care for him. You don't think I am too old?"

"Martha, age and duty are immaterial ideas. If you feel God is urging you to marry, you should obey. Didn't Lazarus say to you 'It will be fine'? Lazarus has looked fear in the face and overcome it. He is telling you to do the same. Oh, yes, sister, we will dance at your wedding!"

Rhoda broke in. "Do you have a suitor? If not, my brother Matthias is available. He's one of Yeshua's followers." All the women laughed.

"I'd be glad to meet him," Martha said, smiling bashfully.

"Wonderful!" Rhoda said. "Then we will really be sisters."

Magdalena breathed a prayer of thanks to God for the abundant love under the Lazarus roof.

In the cool of the evening, Yeshua sat with Peter, Andrew, and Judas on the roof of Lazarus's house. Most of the party had retired to their beds in the house or in the tents they had brought. Passover was still several days off, and the master seemed withdrawn and tired. Peter caught Andrew's eye asking if he should raise a question. Andrew nodded.

"Master, we think your wife is overstepping her role. You are the healer. What was she doing going around the room with her potions, rubbing them on everybody? I thought it was immodest."

"Peter, there are many kinds of healing. She has hers, and I have mine. Both are worthy. Since hers are homely and intimate, they work better on some people than on others. Let her be. I lose nothing by it, and neither do you."

"But I think that the men do lose something by it. She is showing us up. We aren't healers; we are just followers."

"Peter, you will be healers soon enough. Why must you waste the time we have left on arguments about who is better?"

"What do you mean, lord?"

"Again and again I have told you that I will be leaving you soon. You seem to have ears on your heads, but I wonder if they work."

"What? Where are you going?"

"Somewhere you can't follow me. That's why you need to learn all I have to teach because you will be on your own after I'm gone, and it will be up to you to spread the good news of the realm all over the world."

"Not to the pagans and foreigners, surely."

"Yes, Peter, to all of them."

"Not to the Samaritans. Not to the slaves. Not to

Romans."

"Yes, to all of them. I also command you to love all of them, even the ones you call enemies. There are no enemies, only other children of God."

"No, master, this is too much," Judas broke in. "You are the Messiah, and you are here to drive out the Romans so we can have our land back."

"Judas, have you really not heard a word I have said to you? When have I talked of war?"

Judas looked abashed but replied, "Never, but I assumed that was our goal. We rallied all those men in Galilee to march south with you. That's what I told them. I said you were just being figurative in all your speeches about the kingdom. What you really mean is the kingdom of Israel once we drive out the Romans."

Yeshua shook his head. "We will conquer the Romans, but it won't look like you picture it. I am tired. Get some rest, and we will talk more tomorrow." As he descended the steps, Magdalena arose from the bottom step where she had been listening. She took his hand, kissed it, and led him to their tent behind Lazarus' house.

"It will be fine," she said. "Lazarus told me so." Her husband smiled down on her, sadness in his eyes.

———— • ————

The Lazarus house was near the groves on the hill called Olivet. After teaching the disciples in the morning, Yeshua needed a rest and connection to God. He walked up the hill, looking for a large, shady olive tree like the one he prayed under at Capernaum. Magdalena went with him always, and sometimes Levi, Zeno, Eunice, and some of the other women. They circled the tree and sat in peace for as long as God held them. Energized and healed, they returned to the house ready for another lesson.

"What sort of prayer is that?" Martha asked Magdalena as she entered the kitchen door where Martha had been watching the others on the hillside.

"There is no name for it. You could call it the prayer of quiet. Join us, Martha. It may help you let go of that annoyance you feel over your sister and brother. It has made me much more patient."

"Do you pray like that every day?"

"Yes, several times. Whenever Yeshua needs to recover from pouring out his wisdom into us weak vessels. All his energy and knowledge come from God. He couldn't do this on his own. He is teaching us to rely on God, not on our own strength."

Martha's eyes widened. "I do everything on my own strength."

"That's probably why you are so annoyed. You feel used and tired, am I right?"

"Yes." Martha looked down, thinking. "I will join you next time you go up Olivet."

"I will be sure to come and get you," Magdalena said, clasping Martha to her side. After that, Martha became one of the prayer circle, and Magdalena watched her grow more calm and loving over the next few days. This boded well for Martha's future marriage, should such an event take place.

As Passover neared, Yeshua needed to pray more often. Teaching about the realm to students who didn't all absorb his words frustrated him. He needed the reassurance his connection to God gave him. Patiently, he kept teaching and loving his disciples, trusting that God's plan would work out.

Finally, the day came when he would go to the temple

in the huge metropolis of Jerusalem. He sent for a donkey to ride on when the procession of his followers arrived at Bethphage.

"Master, don't you want us to look for a horse or even a mule? You are the messiah. You deserve a taller mount to announce your importance. You will look like a nobody on a donkey," Peter said.

"Always concerned with appearances, Peter. The donkey will fulfill the scriptures. That's much more important than what I look like. Peter, I tell you again to let go of the things of the world."

Peter looked down, ashamed. Just then, Zeno and Levi arrived leading the donkey. When Yeshua sat astride it, his feet almost touched the ground on either side. He looked rather ridiculous to the unbelievers who saw him, but his followers saw an aura of divine light emanating around him. In spite of his humble mount, the master carried the mien of a king. As his followers streamed up the main road to the city, others joined the parade. Excitement grew, and some laid coats and blankets on the road in front of Yeshua. Others broke branches from nearby trees and threw them in front of him. As the donkey trod the branches, the aroma of cedar and pine arose to perfume the air. Magdalena, who tried to stay close to her husband though the crowd jostled her, rejoiced in the smell. Surely God was blessing Yeshua's mission.

Slowing their pace as the road narrowed to enter the temple precincts, suddenly they broke into song. The tune was well known to all the Jews in the crowd, and the volume swelled. Roman soldiers stood at attention, watching the goings-on warily. Passover always brought rowdy crowds into the city, and the fact that the Passover celebrated the Jews' liberation from Egyptian oppression always put people's nerves on edge. What if the Jews took the presence of large crowds of Jews as an opportunity to start an insurrection against the Romans? Tensions ran high any time the city was this busy. No cause for alarm at this point. Besides, the guards kept well away from the temple itself. That was the priests' jurisdiction. If the city streets erupted in violence, the soldiers would intervene, but not inside the temple unless the priests invited them.

Lining the path to the temple proper were stalls for vendors and money changers. Visitors from far-flung towns needed to buy animals to offer in the temple, and to pay for them they had to change their Roman money for temple currency. Unclean Roman coin was not allowed in the holy temple. Customers crowded around these stalls, doing business that the temple required. Magdalena looked at the master and saw a look she had never seen before.

Yeshua swung his leg over the donkey's back and strode directly to a money-changers' table, lifting it up and spilling coins all over the ground. The vendor shouted at him and gestured with his arms. But Yeshua was not stopping to chat. He proceeded down the row of stalls, tipping tables and tossing birdcages over his shoulder to crash open on the path. Peter and Andrew threw punches at the men who attacked, landing a few blows that drew blood. This was more like the war they were anticipating.

"This is a place of prayer, not a place of business. Take this garbage out of my father's house!" the master shouted, though the chaotic yells and curses of the crowd drowned out his voice. Only those nearest heard his words, but everyone saw the anger on his face. Magdalena's eyes filled with tears, but she sniffed them back. Was this the beginning of the end?

When the angry vendors had packed up all their gear and vacated the street, the master took a seat and gathered an audience to hear him teach. For the rest of the day he enthralled his listeners, except the chief priests with their folded arms who stood in the back glaring disapproval at Yeshua. They could have arrested him on the spot, but they bided their time. His clarity and authority impressed the listeners, even some of the temple elders. Magdalena felt a cold thrill up her spine, and she knew those men were her husband's doom. If she had really been a witch, she would have cast a curse their way, but all she could do was pray for mercy on her beloved. All day she sat near him, listening and encouraging him. When evening fell, their company of disciples arose to walk the two miles back to Bethany. The crowd of listeners would have gladly sat there all night to hear more of the good news. This man was a joy to listen to, not at all like the rabbis they were used to hearing, mealy-mouthed and dull.

Chapter 7

Last

The next day, Yeshua asked Magdalena to make the preparations for the Passover celebration. With the helping hands of Martha, Eunice, Zeno, Levi, and Rhoda, she was able to secure a spacious room in the city where they could have a feast together. The city was overcrowded with folks doing the same thing, so Martha and the women cooked all the foods in Bethany and packed them for travel. Sophia and the cart could carry the load, including wine jugs, washing bowls, towels and water. Martha knew the city caterers would be overwhelmed and unreliable. Magdalena made sure to tuck in the alabaster jar full of spikenard oil she had prepared back in Magdala.

Sitting under the big tree on Olivet with the prayer circle, Magdalena saw and felt a disturbing vision. Eyes closed in prayer, she felt a sharp pain in her hand. When she looked at her hand with her inward eye, there was a huge nail driven through it. Raising it in supplication to the master, she saw that his brow was bleeding from a twisted switch of thorns around his head. As she stared into his sad eyes, trickles of blood trailed down her own face, turning the vision crimson. She started and opened her eyes. There were all her friends, eyes closed, sitting peacefully in the half light. All were alive, none were bleeding. She took a deep breath to dispel the pain she felt, giving it over to the unseen taker of worry and fear. Magdalena wouldn't tell Yeshua what she saw. He knew it all anyway. No need to lay her weakness upon him.

About midday, the festive party set off with Sophia pulling her laden cart to return to the city. On the outskirts by a crossroads, Yeshua stopped and gave directions to smaller groups. Zeno and Magdalena would take Sophia by one route, the rest of the women would use a side road that entered the city by a lesser gate, and the men would follow the master.

"Why are we splitting up, Master?" Andrew asked.

"We have aroused too much suspicion among the Pharisees and the priests. I'd rather they didn't see us entering the city and the building we are to dine in. Let's all arrive at different times and try not to call attention."

Andrew and Peter looked quizzically at each other, but said nothing. Was this the same messiah who made a big show of entering the city a few days before?

The dining room they had hired was upstairs, so all the food and supplies had to be carried up the steps. Zeno saw to that while Magdalena bustled to set the tables, cushions, wash bowls, towels, and lamps in place. The upstairs room was already furnished with a long table and several small, low tables for dining from floor cushions. Magdalena and Zeno pushed the long table against one wall and placed the low tables in a circle with the cushions around them. The master had specified that he wanted a circle on one level, nothing to elevate anyone above another, even himself.

"Will we set aside a separate section for the women to eat, my lady?" Zeno asked.

"Oh, no. The master wants women and men to sit together, wives with husbands, sisters with brothers. No separation."

Zeno shook his head, incredulous. "Some of the men will not like that."

"And I know which men those will be," Magdalena smiled.

The other women arrived later by their circuitous route, and they pitched in to set the food out on the tables. Her busyness kept Magdalena from thinking about her vision, but once the work was done and Yeshua arrived with his closest disciples, she had a hard time keeping tears from her eyes. A strong, heavy feeling of finality weighed her down. She kept hearing the words "the last" in her head.

Peter had not brought his wife on the Jerusalem trip. At first, he seemed dismayed to learn that Yeshua wanted husbands and wives to dine together, then he seemed dismayed to realize he had no wife present to dine with. He took a seat alone and found Martha sitting next to him. On her other side was Rhoda's unmarried brother, Matthias. Martha was smiling into Matthias' face. A little spark of gladness shone in Magdalena's heavy heart when she saw love budding.

Yeshua nodded to Magdalena, and the two of them went to the long table. They both wrapped towels around their waists and picked up wash bowls filled with water. Beginning with Peter, the master went around the room, knelt by each of his disciples, and washed his feet, drying with the towel. Magdalena followed him, mirroring his actions for the women disciples. Some of the men smiled, some flinched at the master's touch, and some couldn't bear to look at Yeshua. The women gladly received Magdalena's ministrations. Such pampering came seldom in their lives as they devoted themselves to serving others, not being served. Magdalena noticed that Mother Mary and Martha had tears in their eyes as they smiled their gratitude. When she and Yeshua put the bowls and towels away and returned to sit side by side in the circle, the master spoke.

"My beloved friends, in all that I do I am showing you how to live. In washing your feet I model what I want you to do for each other. Humble yourself and serve your brother and sister. It's not about conquering enemies, it's about doing good for others. The enemy you all need to overcome is that pride that speaks evil within you. The poison comes from within, not without. When you can make the inside like the outside---clean--- then you will understand my words."

Magdalena watched the gathered disciples. Some had their eyes fixed on Yeshua and seemed to be listening. Some picked at the food laid before them, even though no one had said the blessing. A couple of young men were slapping each other playfully, teasing about some secret joke. No wonder Yeshua was frustrated so often. Did they not understand how special this night was? Magdalena wanted to observe every detail of every moment and freeze it in her mind. Maybe she could preserve it, just as it was, so she could relive it later, when her husband was gone. As soon as she conceived the thought she realized its futility. Nothing lasted in the face of time. This night would pass away. She had to let it.

Yeshua blessed the food and broke the bread. Then he picked up a cup of wine and spoke a speech that brought many in the room to tears.

"Think of this, my brothers and sisters. I am a grapevine. I have many living branches stretching out into the world. You are those branches. My love and my words flow out into you, and you live and produce fruit. That fruit is food and drink for the world. If my love can't flow into you, the branch will die and no more fruit will come. If a branch is torn off, the same thing results. If, however, you stay with me, the vine, all will be well. Life and love come in the flow of my union with you.

"Now, I am going to leave you, but the vine of my word and your memory of it will stay with you. Let my power continue to feed you, and you will still produce fruit. After I am gone from your presence, think of me every time you drink the wine. It will remind you of my word and my love, and we will be connected again. I will be in you, you will be in me, we will be one, never to be separated." He lifted his cup, and all the gathered friends lifted theirs. Magdalena saw the aura of green light around the heads of some of the followers when they drank the wine. Their faces showed they had felt a different energy in that sip, the connection Yeshua spoke of. The wine was more than usual wine; it was Yeshua's love in liquid form.

Magdalena leaned her head onto her husband's chest and sobbed quietly. He encircled her with his arm and kissed her hair. How much longer would she have to hold him? She tried not to think of the "last" and kept her mind and heart on the moment of love and closeness.

The banquet continued, and as more wine was

drunk, the hilarity increased. Laughter and smiles lit the room as food was shared and stories were told.

"Tell us, Master, which one of us do you love the most?" Peter called across the room from his seat. "We have a bet on." He swigged another mouthful of wine and smiled as if the question were a joke.

"Yes, tell us," Andrew said. "I'm sure it's me." Suddenly the room grew still as revelers realized what was happening. Tension took over. What would Yeshua say? Magdalena saw that several of the women were looking at her.

Magdalena tossed her hair over her shoulder, lifted her body to its full height, and with a smirk on her face called out, "Oh, that's easy. It's me of course!" and kissed Yeshua full on the mouth in front of everyone. Laughter broke out after a slight pause, defusing the tension. Then she arose from the floor and went to the long table to retrieve the jar of oil she had brought. Kneeling on the floor behind the master, she anointed his hair with the perfumed oil, and the earthy, soothing scent of spikenard flowed through the room. Slowly and adoringly she stroked the oil through his locks, massaged it into his neck and shoulders, then onto his hands and arms. His feet and legs she also anointed. All the time her tears flowed quietly down her cheeks. Reverently the women watched, praying in their hearts. Most of them had anointed the bodies of the dead and knew it was a solemn rite.

"What a waste," Judas said. "A jar that size could have been sold to feed the poor." Some of the men grumbled in agreement.

"Leave her alone. She is preparing me for death," Yeshua said. "The time for my betrayal is at hand."

"Who would ever betray you, Master? I certainly

wouldn't," Andrew said.

"Nor would I," Peter exclaimed. "Who are you talking about?"

Magdalena noticed that Judas said nothing.

"All of you, one way or another, will betray me. But even a branch broken from the vine can be grafted back in. Return to me, and I will flow through you again, always, to the end of time."

Yeshua called Judas to his side and whispered in his ear. Judas nodded, with a stricken look on his face, and left the room. Magdalena's stomach tightened as she remembered her vision regarding Judas. She felt a cataclysmic change nearing.

"I need to pray," Yeshua said and arose from his seat. Magdalena, considering her role, hesitated. Should she go with the master or stay with the women to clean up the food and dishes? Her eyes met Martha's, and Martha mouthed the words 'go with him.' She threw her veil around her neck and hurried to catch up with her husband and the other disciples.

Walking beside Yeshua, hand in hand, Magdalena felt how agitated he was. The Passover dinner had drained him of power and filled him with dread. He needed to connect to God for strength and reassurance. They didn't speak; she just walked with him, hoping her love could carry him for a while. When they arrived at Olivet, he told the disciples to wait for him but stay watchful. He wanted to be alone with God and walked off away from view. The men flopped down on the ground and immediately went to sleep, snoring in their drunken state. The only man still awake was Levi. He and Magdalena agreed silently to follow the master but to keep hidden. They found Yeshua lying prostrate under his favorite olive tree, crying out and pounding his fists in the dust. After letting out some anger, he sat up and assumed his prayer posture with palms open. The green light surrounded him, and for a while he seemed to be praying peacefully. Then Magdalena and Levi noticed a change in his face. In the moonlight, a red film clouded his countenance, and Magdalena remembered the dream in which blood had flowed down her face and his. Her heart ached to go to him, to comfort him, but she kept her station in the dark. When her husband made a move to rise, she and Levi returned to the sleeping disciples. Still they snored, but they awoke suddenly when voices of a mob entered the olive grove. A dozen temple police, armed with spears and swords approached, led by Judas and several of the priests and Pharisees. Groggy, the disciples jumped up and drew their swords to defend the master who was just walking up after his prayer. Judas approached and kissed Yeshua.

"Greetings, Master." Though his voice mimicked cheerfulness, his troubled face told another story.

Magdalena tried to keep near Yeshua, but the police pulled him away from her. In a daze, she followed them back into Jerusalem where her husband was locked away in a cell in the temple complex. She wanted to sit there all night, but Levi persuaded her to return to Bethany where Martha could comfort her. Fitfully she slept inside the Lazarus house under Martha's loving care. Oddly, her tears had stopped flowing.

Chapter 8

Cross

"Martha, I must be near him. I promised never to leave him."

"Magdalena, it's not safe for any of us to go into the city. The temple police will be all over the place, and who knows if the Romans won't also be on alert."

"Have any of the men shown up, besides Levi and Zeno?"

"No, they scattered and went underground. Nobody has seen any of them."

"Where have the guards taken Yeshua?"

"Somewhere in the temple."

"That's a huge place. Do we know anyone among the Pharisees who is sympathetic? What about that Nicodemus who used to sneak over to talk to the master? Yes, I will go find him. Don't tell me no, sister. I must do this."

Martha's face fell, but she kissed Magdalena and

wished her well.

"We mustn't let fear steal our time, right? I think you told me that."

Magdalena smiled, and started her lonely walk to the city in search of Nicodemus. As she neared the temple, her courage waned. Who could she ask? She risked arrest herself if anyone knew she was married to the master. "I can't do this alone," she said to herself. She stopped under a shaded wall, sat down and opened her heart and hands. "Beloved, show me the way," she breathed. Her vision smelled of rotten eggs. She looked down on the healing pool of Theon and beside the edge of the pool sat a pair of red cloth slippers, embroidered with silver thread. Instantly she knew where to find the man she sought and how to identify him when she found him. "Thank you, Love," she said, arose and headed to the healing pool.

She peered through the opening in the wall surrounding the healing pool. The sulfur in the steaming spring emitted foul fumes like those she had smelled in her vision. Half a dozen men, most of them elderly, were bobbing in the bath. Achy joints and stiff limbs improved in the hot, smelly water. She waited patiently for one of the men to emerge and put on the red slippers. When he stepped out into the street, she accosted him.

"Sir, I am Magdalena, the wife of Yeshua the teacher. I wonder if you can tell me where he has been taken."

Nicodemus looked furtively around, then led her into a side street where they could speak without being observed. "How did you know how to find me?"

"Your fancy slippers."

"Yes, my brother the shoemaker made them for me. My colleagues laugh at me, but the slippers cheer my heart, so I wear them. Your husband went before the Sanhedrin this morning, and they handed him over to Pilate. They want him executed."

"What can I do to save him?" she asked, her woman's heart coming to the fore, even though she knew the outcome Yeshua had foretold.

"Traditionally, the governor releases one condemned prisoner to please the crowd at Passover. Pilate will speak from the balcony of his palace. If you can muster enough voices, you might persuade him to release Yeshua, but you will have to be very loud."

"Thank you, and may God bless you, sir. I must go." And Magdalena hurried to Bethany to gather the women, Zeno and Levi. They needed more voices, but the other men were in hiding. Twelve women joined the choir: Magdalena, Mother Mary, Martha, Mary her sister, Eunice, and Rhoda. Six others from the crowd of followers joined them along the road.

"Sisters," Magdalena said as they walked, "we have women's voices, and we need to make them carry to out-shout the crowd. Breathe deep and let your voice arise from down in your body, not just from your throat. That will amplify the sound." Brave and determined, the women agreed, but their courage fled when they saw the size of the throng gathered outside Pilate's balcony. A hundred or more rowdy people shouted and raised their fists insistently.

When Pilate asked, "Who do you want me to release for you?" a roar of "Barabbas" drowned out the feeble "Yeshua" that came from their small choir of voices.

"Are you sure?" Pilate asked again.

The crowd kept shouting "Barabbas."

"Then, what do you want me to do with your king,

Yeshua?"

Magdalena's little band were stunned into silence when the crowd erupted into a chant of "Crucify him! Crucify him!"

"Oh!" Mother Mary sighed, fainting from the shock, the crowd, and the heat. The women gathered around her.

"Give her room to breathe," Martha said.

"Let's get her into a house," Zeno said, lifting the petite woman in his arms.

Just a few doors down, a man welcomed them into his cool parlor. "Bring her in here. Sarah, some water for the lady. Put her on the couch."

Mary recovered with the care of the women, Sarah, and the man of the house whose name was Joseph. She was fed, fanned, and rested.

"What happened? The last thing I heard was the word 'crucify.'"

Rhoda patted her hand. "You fainted, dear Mother."

"She can rest here as long as she needs to. Angry crowds like that could make anyone faint," Joseph said.

"It's her son," Rhoda said.

Joseph looked more closely at the woman he had taken into his house. His face betrayed recognition. "Oh, my dear sister. My house is yours. Bless you, and God bless your innocent son. Are you all his followers?"

The women nodded. Zeno had gone to the door to keep watch for Levi who had remained behind to hear what would be done with Yeshua.

"Here's Levi. What is Pilate's decision?"

"They will be taking him to the place of the skull. The Romans are in charge of him now, and they've been ordered to arrest any of his followers they find skulking about."

"That means you, all of you," Joseph said, shaking his head. "If you need a place to hide, you are welcome here. I heard your teacher talk in the temple one day. He has the words of the living God. I want to help you any way I can."

"Thank you. I, for one, will go to the place of the skull," Magdalena said. "I must be with him to the end. The Romans won't arrest a woman. I am beneath their contempt, invisible."

"I will accompany you, daughter," Mother Mary said.

Rhoda and Martha tried to dissuade her, but Yeshua's mother was determined.

"Zeno, at least bring the donkey so she needn't walk all that way. You will need to save what strength you have, Mother."

The older woman smiled her gratitude. When Zeno arrived with Sophia, Mother Mary rode the donkey, led by Martha and Magdalena, down to the place of the skull, where executions were carried out, beyond the city walls but easily visible, as a deterrent to other rebels. They heard the shouts of the crowd surrounding Yeshua on his staggering walk to the crucifixion hill. When he appeared, Magdalena almost didn't recognize him.

He had fallen on his face several times, carrying his own cross, and his face was bloody. One of his eyes was swollen shut. His bloody hair was twisted in the thorn crown they had placed on his head, the thorns digging into his flesh. She had dreamed of that crown. He was naked except for a cloth wrapped around his hips. Magdalena remembered stroking every inch of that body, lovingly in their bed. She couldn't take in the truth of what she was seeing. Flaps of his flesh had been torn open by the flogging whips, and blood streamed out of the gashes. Mother Mary cried out at the sight of him, and Martha and Magdalena had to hold her up. Some people in the crowd threw rocks and clods at him, while others mourned in silence. Yeshua was beaten nearly to death, and the crucifixion seemed unnecessary to many who watched. He was fainting as they fastened him to the wooden cross and lifted it up to set it into its post-hole. He had barely flinched as the nails were driven into his hands and heels, his pain had already been so extreme.

Magdalena drew near. She looked up into his one open eye and caught a glimpse of the man she loved. His head hung down, and he could breathe only shallowly.

"My husband, I am here," she said, keeping her voice level and eyes dry.

"Yes, Mary. Will you take care of my mother? She is now your mother and you are her daughter."

"Yes, my love. What else can I do?"

"Stay awake." His ragged breath was hard for her to hear.

"Woman, be gone from here," a Roman soldier shouted at her, shoving her roughly aside.

She walked back to the spot where Martha tended to Mary. Blackness crept in around the edges of her heart, and she felt her demons making inroads. She took a deep breath and remembered what Yeshua said---that love is stronger than death and they would always be connected, across miles and millennia. As she looked up at him hanging there, she saw a tendril of green light, like a vine, curling across the distance from his heart over to her. When it reached her, it curled around her and filled her heart with comfort and courage. She knew that his love was still alive inside her and around

her. Even as he whispered "It is finished" and sagged
in death, she was upheld by his power and his love. He
was in her and she was in him. They united into one
complete human, made of and sustained by love.

"We should take Mother Mary home, or back to
Joseph's house. She is not well," Martha said.

"Zeno!" Magdalena called. He had been hiding
behind one of the large boulders on the barren hillside.
He came quickly, leading Sophia. "Take Mother Mary
back to Joseph's. I will stay here to see what they do with
the master's body."

What they did first was to stab his side with a
spear to make sure he was dead. Out flowed water and
blood, reminding Magdalena of her dream when she
and Yeshua poured wine and water into a bowl on the
mountain. What did it mean? As a concession to the
Jews in Jerusalem, the Romans allowed the corpses to be
buried, instead of leaving them on the crosses till they
were consumed by scavenger birds. But Magdalena had
no help to take the body away.

Just then she heard her name called and turned to
see Joseph and Nicodemus hurrying up the hill toward
her.

"Let me have his body! I have permission to bury
it," Joseph said. Breathlessly, he conferred with the
Roman guard who nodded and gestured dismissively
that he cared not a whit what was done with the body.
Joseph had brought a donkey cart from his house where
his servant Sarah was caring for Mother Mary. He and
Nicodemus dragged and carried Yeshua's bloody corpse
to the cart and lifted it in.

"We are taking it across to where I have a new
tomb. We will lay him there."

Magdalena said, "I will follow you." The three

trudged to the place Joseph mentioned. Zeno was waiting for them, having been sent on by Sarah. The three men carried the body of Yeshua into the tomb carved in the hillside and laid it out on one of the shelves, wrapping it in a white cloth.

"I'm afraid we have no spices to anoint him," Nicodemus said. "I will send two of my servants with some, when the sabbath is over."

"He has already been anointed," Magdalena said. She sat down on a nearby rock as if she would wait there forever, watching the three faithful followers roll the disc-shaped stone in front of the tomb opening.

"Come, Magdalena. The other women are back at my house. You need rest and food. Come," Joseph urged.

"Thank you, but I must watch here. I promised I would not leave him."

Zeno said, "I will stay here with you, my lady."

"No, dear Zeno. I want to be alone. I am not afraid," and that was all she said. Her silence told them that she would not be moved, so they left her.

Chapter 9

Awake

Magdalena passed the time by observing the night sounds and thanking God for each one of the creatures that made them---the owls, the foxes, the tiny scurrying animals in the underbrush. Then she prayed silently, listening for the voice of God or of her husband. When the sun rose, she observed the waking animals, the rising breeze, the sounds of people beginning work in the city behind the walls. On the sabbath, the Jews were not part of that bustle, being commanded not to work, but there were plenty of non-Jews living in the city to make a noise. She listened for the shouts of men and the rumbling of carts. Even at this distance she could hear babies' cries and domestic animals braying, mooing, and crowing. Life continued in the world around her. Only her husband had died. Everyone else lived. She considered dying herself. She had plenty of fatal herbs at her home in Magdala; she could easily dose herself and end the suffering. But the demon of yearning for death had been driven out of her in the wilderness when she first met Yeshua, and she was stronger now. She could resist that yearning. Whatever lay ahead, she would live it.

As the day grew hotter, she moved with the shade of the tree she sat under. At one location, she noticed an ant hill and the busy ants going in and out of the hole. Those entering carried tiny bits of valuable food. Those leaving carried useless trash that they transported to the edge of the hill and dropped. No ants stood still. No ants sat ruminating or lamenting their lot. Magdalena imagined that all the ants were content, glad to have a purpose, even if it was earth-bound and humble. God loved the ants and had gifted them with purpose and contentment. She knew God loved her, too, but what was her purpose, now that Yeshua was dead? She asked that question in her heart and heard nothing. The answer would come, but she had to wait for it. Patience was a gift she had received lately, since she started praying silently with Yeshua. She could wait.

The sun was dropping lower and the shadows lengthening when she could no longer keep her eyes open. She had fought hunger, thirst, heat, and drowsiness, until now. Her head drooped, and she jerked it up. In her heart she heard the word 'surrender.' Smiling, she rolled her veil into a pillow of sorts, and lay down under the tree. Immediately, she saw the most detailed and protracted vision of her life. Giving into it, she let it take her where it desired. She was with her husband, who wore a white tunic with a golden belt. His hair, matted and bloody on the cross, was shiny clean and flowing. His eyes glowed deep and clear. Suddenly, she felt that she *was* her husband because she was looking out through his eyes and felt his feelings as he felt them.

With him in his body, she felt his muscles pressing against a resistant substance, trying to push through it. It was harder than soil but softer than stone. In his hand, he carried a staff of iron with an end like a chisel which he sometimes used to batter against the wall or chip away at the substance. Willing him to succeed, she added her strength to his and they made some progress, breaking through, first into a cave then into a grotto with an underground stream where they refreshed themselves. Finally, they reached a large cavern like a forecourt. At one end of it stood two huge bronze gates, studded with nail heads and strapped with silver hinges. Through his eyes, she knew this was their destination: the place of the dead. Her heart asked, "Why are we here?"

The answer she heard through him: "Freedom."

When Yeshua thrust the staff against the doors, they thudded with a dull sound. He pounded again and again. Did he expect someone to open them? She felt him call on God for strength, and his prayer was answered. The next stroke caused the doors to fall off their hinges and crash to the ground of the forecourt. More like an explosion, the sound of it shook the earth and echoed through the ground for miles and miles. Looking at the sight through his eyes, Magdalena felt his surprise at what he saw.

The ground of the chamber was lined with white, fuzzy balls or pellets. They stretched as far as the eye could see in all directions, millions and millions of them. Were they sheep? Were they eggs? She realized they were cocoons. Inside each was the soul of a man or woman who had died before the coming of her husband, before they could hear the good news of the realm. He was here to liberate them from their limbo and send them back to God, their source and their salvation.

Yeshua raised his staff and shouted, "Awake! Awake!" He struck the staff on the ground and the impact echoed down the chamber. "Awake, Awake!"

Magdalena looked at the nearest of the cocoons and saw a hole opening in the end. The creature inside had chewed through the silken case. She scanned the miles and miles of cocoons and realized that all those she could see were breaking open in the same way. From each white cocoon emerged a moth. The colors of the moths varied from deep red to yellow to green to pink. On each cocoon, the free soul unrolled its wings, stretched them out, and flew up, drawn to a distant light high above them. Following their flight through Yeshua's eyes, she saw them ascend in a colorful cloud, up and up through the darkness. As they soared further and further into the distance, they became colored specks, like confetti, or like stars in the Milky Way. Her eye followed them until they disappeared into a distance she couldn't reach, and she felt a flood of joy over her heart. She knew they had reached God and returned into love. The uprising of the souls continued, as there were millions of souls to liberate from the moment of creation to the current day: Jews, pagans, unbelievers, prehistoric peoples, people from parts of the world never seen, good people, evil people, children who died in the womb, elders who died full of years, women, men, eunuchs. Up they all flew, returning to their source.

When the swarm of moth souls stopped ascending, she saw through Yeshua's eyes that there were a few unopened cocoons still lying inert on the ground. Yeshua shouted, "Awake!" to them. No response. Again he shouted. Nothing. He went to them, and through his arm, Magdalena felt the softness of the cocoon when Yeshua tapped it with his staff and shouted "Awake!" again. Still no response.

A tall, dark figure hovered out of the blackness and spoke in a flat, deep voice:

"It's no use. They don't want to go."

Yeshua said, "Greetings, Serapis. I must try with every soul."

"Yes, I know. You are very good that way. But if the soul refuses your ministrations, it stays here, blind and trapped. Would you like me to show you the state they are in? I can give you a glimpse inside one of the cocoons."

Magdalena yearned to see inside one of the cocoons, but Yeshua hesitated. Finally, he said, "Yes, show me."

At a gesture of Serapis's hand, the fuzzy surface of the nearest inert cocoon became transparent, and Magdalena could see inside what looked like a slug or a maggot---a legless blob of matter with no face or distinguishable shape. She recoiled from its ugliness.

"The torments of this place, the loneliness, the darkness, the regret, the fear, the emptiness---none of it has caused this soul to change. No growth, no transformation, no repentance. And if you ask them to come with you, they refuse. They think they are right. To change would be admitting defeat, and they are too stubborn to do that. Their essence is still under the control of their human vanity. They have gone backward, to a slug-like form. It's futile."

"But I had no chance to warn them."

"You are not the only savior, Lord. God tried to save them, even if they didn't acknowledge the name of God. Their consciences, placed inside them by God,

93

tried to save them. Even their own human hearts could have saved them if they had only loved. You can't save everyone."

Yeshua sighed and said, "You speak wisdom, Serapis. I have done what I can here. I have further tasks to carry out before I can return to God myself. Farewell."

"Farewell, brother. Leave these poor fools to my care. Give my love to God."

"I shall."

Then the vision changed location, as dreams do, and Magdalena found herself, still looking through Yeshua's eyes, in a bridal chamber filled with candlelight. The warm aromas of incense and candle wax surrounded her, and she saw red cushions embroidered with gold thread, lush amethyst curtains at the windows, and an intricate patterned carpet beneath her bare feet. She took a sip of the sweet wine in the goblet she held and turned to look at the large bed . On the bed lay a beautiful woman clad in only a diaphanous shift, her hair trailing across the pillow. One arm was above her head, and the other was across her belly. Her wrist wore the sapphire bracelet Magdalena had sent to market with Zeno and Levi. She realized she was looking at herself on the bed through the eyes of her beloved. A confused mixture of shock and fascination thrilled through her. What was about to happen?

She moved toward the bed and lay down next to herself. Through Yeshua's fingers, she felt the texture of her own hair as he stroked it gently. She felt the smoothness of her own skin as he ran his rougher hand over her breast, belly, and hips. At the same time, she felt his hand on her from inside her own skin. She was within him and without him at once. Her mind could barely fathom the double nature of the sensations she was feeling, so she willed herself to stay inside Yeshua's body. She had never been there before, while she knew well how her own body felt and responded. As him, she saw how beautiful and appealing she was. Inside him, she felt his desire rise and his heart pounding. For a moment, fear made her doubt, and she considered reining in the vision, but then she surrendered to the ride it took her on. She was a man. She was in love with a beautiful woman, and she was making love to her. The strength of her husband's drive took her breath away. She surged forward on a wave of power and felt the sensation he felt when he entered her. Her female insides were soft and yielding to her male force. Enlightenment broke through in the process. This is what men felt. This is why they acted as they did. She willed herself to stay with her husband's perception, and suddenly she went deep within him. She felt the explosion of his release and then she became one of his seeds, swimming in irresistible propulsion up and up the wet tunnel of her own body. She had only one goal: to reach the egg. When her bullet head bumped up against the egg, she butted it with all her strength. She pushed and drilled and battered and shoved until she broke through the egg's surface. Then she was spinning. Colors swirled around her and she spun with them. Dizzy and lost, she cried out. Then she opened her eyes.

Chapter 10

Room

Yeshua looked down at her as she lay with her head on her rolled up veil in the morning light under the tree. She knew she was in the real world because of the pain in her back and the morning songs of birds, but her husband still wore the shreds of dream. Half ghost and half man, his body glowed and his features shaded in and out of focus. Love flowed out of his eyes from a depth she had never plumbed.

"That must have been quite a dream," he said.

"I went with you to free the dead."

"I know."

"Was that real?"

"Yes. One of my tasks. But I am not done. I have a little over a month to finish teaching and set the disciples on their paths. You can help me. You will find them holed up in the upper room where we ate supper. They're hiding from the police. Go and tell them I am risen and I will meet them over the next few days."

"You still want them? They abandoned you, almost to a man. Only Levi, Zeno, Nicodemus, and Joseph can be trusted among the men. That is Joseph's tomb where we laid you." She gestured to the tomb and saw that the stone was lying flat on the ground just like the doors of the underworld had been after Yeshua blasted them down.

"Yes, I still want them. Unlike you, they never understood me when I spoke, but now they will. They have changed."

"May I hold you, my love?"

"Yes, but you won't like it," he said.

She put her arms around him as she usually did, but he felt slight, incorporeal. Not the strong man she had lived inside during the vision. She let her arms drop.

"I am in a between state until I return to God. Try to remember me the way I was in your vision."

"Was that real?"

"More real than anything you have lived so far. That is what I meant by making the male and female one, united, undivided. Did you feel it?"

"Oh, yes, and I think I understand men better now."

"You should understand God better now, too. How did you see yourself from inside my eyes?"

"I was beautiful, worthy, and totally lovable."

"That is how God and I see you. That is how we see everybody. And God is telling everybody that constantly. It's only the world that tells people different, and the double-minded listen to the world. The unified listen to God."

"Can we stay here all day? I don't want you to leave."

"No, people will be coming to anoint my body. Don't let the demon of craving back in, Mary. You know not to cling, even to me. You will see me again, and after I am gone, you will always hear from me--."

"If I have ears."

"Right." He smiled. "Now, off to tell the others what you have seen. The tomb is open and I am not there."

"I love you, Yeshua. Good bye." She wanted to cry, but she wanted to obey her husband more. Maybe she had changed, too. She ran as fast as the uneven ground allowed and went directly to the upper room.

When she knocked, she heard hushed voices and feet scrabbling on the wooden floor. No one answered. They must be hiding.

"It's me, Magdalena. Let me in!" she called, knocking again. Eventually, the door opened a crack and Andrew peeked out. Confirming it was her, he opened the door just enough to admit her and barred it again.

"I have seen the master. He is risen like he said. He sent me to tell you."

"We must go to him!" Peter said.

"He may or may not be there, but you can see the empty tomb. He said to tell you he will come to you."

"Where? Where shall we meet him?"

"Be patient. He will find you. No need to chase around looking for him."

"But some of us ran off to Emmaus, and some have headed home to Capernaum. Only a few of us are still in the city."

"Yes, he will find all of the disciples, wherever they are. Time and space mean nothing to him now. He will meet us all, over the next few days. Just wait."

"Wait! How can we wait?" And two of the disciples raced out of the room. They hadn't asked Magdalena for directions to the tomb, but they ran wildly in a passion to see the master. Magdalena wondered if they had changed very much. They looked like competitive puppies still.

"Lock the door behind them," Thomas said. "The watch is due to make its round. We need to be quiet till they pass."

Magdalena didn't mind being still. She helped herself to a drink of water and ate some dates, the first food she had eaten since Thursday night. Closing her eyes, she went to that center of stillness she so enjoyed, and waited.

When a rhythmic, secret knock came at the door, Thomas opened it to admit Peter, John, and Levi.

Peter said, "We saw the tomb and the winding sheet. That old spy Nicodemus was there and a lot of other people. No sign of the master, though. I guess we will have to wait. Is there anything to eat?" Magdalena resisted the urge to serve him. She stayed put. After a little while of eating and resting, the disciples saw the master appear in the room. There had been no knock, and no one had admitted him. He shimmered all in white and gold, but still they knew him.

"Peace, everyone," he said. The disciples' faces registered shock, all except Magdalena's.

"Master, we went to look for you, but you had gone. Are you really alive?" John asked.

"Can we touch you?" Thomas asked.

"If you wish," Yeshua said.

Thomas took the blurry hand of his teacher and put his finger on the mark of the nail. His brow wrinkled. "I don't know. You are different." He dropped the hand and backed away.

"Fear not, beloved. All will be well. I am just here to answer any questions and reassure you of your mission."

"Teacher, I don't think I was listening when you

talked about sin. Could you tell us that again?"

"Yes," said Yeshua. "There is no such thing as sin, as such. You create the sin yourself when you cheat on your true self with the things of the world. You forget the good within you and you chase after illusions you think are real. Sin doesn't exist outside of you."

"But doesn't death come from sin?"

"Death and sickness come from craving things that are bad for you. If you could be content at heart, undivided, you would not become sick."

"Can peace be found in this life, or only in the next?"

"The child of true humanity is within you, your true self, the one you have been since before you were born. If you search for it, you will find it. When you find it, you will have peace in this life."

"What is the 'child of true humanity'?"

"The true human is the whole human. No divisions, no cravings for what is not, no self-importance. Nothing splits the heart; the entire heart is focused on giving and receiving love, not on fame, wealth, power, or adulation. This is the good news I want you to teach."

"And you want us to teach it all over?"

"Yes, all over the world, as far as you can reach. Oh, and just stick to the message I gave you. Don't go adding a lot of rules and laws that you made up. They will just trap you later."

The disciples looked dubious. The master arose and walked to the door. Raising his hand in benediction he said, "I leave my peace with you all. I must be off. I have meetings right now in Emmaus and in Capernaum." And he passed through the door without opening it.

In stunned silence, the disciples looked at each other. John got up and paced the room, wringing his hands. Andrew sat with his head in his hands, crying quietly.

Peter attacked Thomas for asking to touch the master. It was all emotion and chaos.

"We can't go out preaching! They'll kill us!"

"We can't trust anybody, the Pharisees, the Romans, the priests and their police. Where can we hide?"

Magdalena intervened with the calmest voice she could muster.

"Fear not, my brothers. We should praise the master for teaching us the way to wholeness. We must tell of his greatness and wisdom. We mustn't waste time on fear."

"Sister," asked Peter, "did he teach you anything he didn't teach to us? You spent time alone with him. What did he say?"

"Yes, I don't mind sharing his words. He once praised me for not being upset when I saw a vision of him. The word he used was 'wavering.' He praised me for not wavering. Steadfastness and endurance. That's what he wants from us."

Levi said, "Well, you sure showed steadfastness the night they crucified him." Magdalena smiled shyly at the compliment, but Peter looked fierce.

"Anything else?" Thomas asked.

"He taught me the names of the seven powers of wrath and how to overcome them. He said that freeing oneself from those powers brings peace and rest."

Andrew spoke up, "I never heard him teach these ideas. They are strange. I don't believe he said that."

"And I don't believe he would reveal secret teachings to a woman," Peter said. "Would the master choose a mere woman over us and sneak off to teach her in private?"

"Brothers, what do you think of me? Are you saying I made up bogus teachings myself and I am passing them off as my husband's? Why would I do that?"

Levi jumped to Magdalena's defense. "Peter, you have such a temper. If Yeshua says she is worthy, she is. We have no cause to doubt her and her words. I, for one, intend to put on the clothing of the whole human and go out to preach the word of love and peace." As he arose, Levi looked around the room to see who would join him. Magdalena and Thomas followed him out the door and down the stairs, leaving Peter and Andrew to stew.

"Where will you go?" Magdalena asked her brothers at the bottom of the steps.

"The closest place the master mentioned is Emmaus," said Thomas. "Care to accompany me?"

"I must go to the home of Joseph. Mother Mary is there with Martha and some other women. After that, I will return to Magdala. You are both welcome at my home any time."

"It looks like the branches are torn off the vine," Levi said.

"Don't despair, my dear brother. The master is always with us, across any distance. We can always contact him. Come with me to Joseph's. Zeno will feed us."

Levi smiled and went with Magdalena after embracing Thomas in farewell.

When they reached Joseph's house, Zeno met them at the door with a dark expression on his face.

"Has something happened, Zeno? It's not Mother Mary, is it?" Magdalena asked.

"No, it's Judas. He hanged himself."

Her vision of a figure hanging from a tree flashed on Magdalena's mind. She had foreseen it.

Levi said, "Can things get any worse?"

Zeno spat on the ground. "Don't say that. You will bring on more sorrow."

Martha approached and embraced Magdalena.

"Mother Mary is feeling much better. Joseph has fed us all and given us rest. We should return to Bethany as soon as possible. Lazarus has been waiting on himself all these days."

"Of course. Zeno, bring Sophia around." The party thanked Joseph for his hospitality and bid him and Sarah farewell. Walking home to Bethany was a silent trek, not at all like the festive parade they had marched in with palm leaves and songs a few days before. Shock and exhaustion tied their tongues.

More sadness met them at the Lazarus house. They found Lazarus in bed, weak and near death, his heart broken by the news of Yeshua's crucifixion.

"Welcome home," he whispered in a dry rasp. "Now I can go. I have waited to say good-bye to you, my dear sisters. With the master gone, I want to go, too. I have no fear."

Tears and remonstration couldn't change Lazarus's decision. He smiled as they kissed his cheek, and he died.

"What will we do now?" Mary asked her sister. Martha shook her head.

"Come to me in Magdala," Magdalena said. I have a big house. Sell this house and live with me. Mother Mary is living with me, too." The sisters couldn't answer, but there was a spark of interest in Martha's eye. Magdalena would wait for their answer, but she wouldn't wait in Bethany. She yearned to be back by the shores of Galilee, the site of her early happiness with Yeshua. The next day, she and Zeno packed up the donkey cart and set off to the north. The crowds of followers who had trailed behind them when they arrived had long since dispersed. Their tiny band consisted of Mother Mary, Magdalena, Zeno, and Sophia.

Chapter 11

Magdala

A few days before the new moon, Mother Mary addressed Magdalena.

"Daughter, should we be preparing for New Moon School? I hope you will resume your teaching."

"Oh, Mother, I have no enthusiasm for it."

"The local women are counting on it, you know. You are such a blessing to them, and Yeshua would want you to keep telling the good news. Your demons of darkness are not attacking you again, are they?"

"Not really. I am just so tired."

"Then maybe it's something else."

"Like what?"

"Like a baby, perhaps?" Mother Mary gave her an arch look.

Magdalena's eyes widened in surprise. She had barely begun to sense a change in her body, the change she recognized from her previous pregnancy.

Mary laughed. "Don't look so shocked. I've been around lots of pregnant women, and I've had babies of my own. I can read the signs. Tiredness is a big one. I am very happy."

Tears shone in Magdalena's eyes. "Yeshua will never see his son or daughter."

"Yes, he will, in spirit. And we will have a little piece of him to live with us here. It's a miracle."

Magdalena didn't tell her how much of a miracle it was. She had not slept with her husband since her last bleeding, except in the vision at the tomb side. If she was with child, it was a supernatural conception.

"Mother, we must keep it a secret. The child will inherit the father's enemies." Mother Mary looked concerned. She had only thought of the joy, not the danger.

"We will pray about it to God. God will protect the child." She laid a reassuring hand on Magdalena's shoulder. "So, what about the school?"

"Yes, we will have school, but let's hope no one else has eyes as sharp as yours."

"For safety, wear your loosest tunic," Mary smiled.

Word went out that New Moon School would resume, and the local women made food and washed their garments. Some of their husbands, missing the master, asked if they could attend. Magdalena said yes. Since Yeshua's death, the disciples had scattered and were spreading the good news in their own ways in various regions. Many of them stayed near Jerusalem since there was a larger concentration of people there to preach to. But some had returned to their villages and towns, meeting in the homes of believers secretly. Following the teaching of Yeshua was declared illegal and anyone caught could be arrested and killed. Since they called him "King of the Jews," he was a threat to the emperor and therefore a traitor. So were all his followers.

Magdalena's school had met long before the public and infamous crucifixion of the master, and most people considered it a witch school anyway. No one thought a bunch of crazy women were a threat, so the monthly meeting wasn't scrutinized. Ironically, as divisions grew between the various preaching groups, men and women came to Magdalena's to hear the words of the master. They trusted her for several reasons: she had been the master's wife, she had been the first to see him risen, and she had never abandoned him. Who better to convey the teachings accurately? Zeno warned her about letting outsiders into the school. They might be spies. But Magdalena chose to persist in sharing her husband's teachings to all who cared to hear.

As women started arriving at her house, Magdalena greeted them and directed them to the courtyard. Mother Mary took charge of any children and led them to the nursery room. Looking down the road, Magdalena spotted two donkeys approaching carrying two women. Her heart began to race, and she called out to them.

"Martha! Mary! God be praised, I am so happy to see you. Are you here to stay?"

The women smiled as they dismounted before her door.

"We have lots of news, Magdalena," Martha said. "We can tell you later, when you are not so busy."

"No, sisters, tell me now!"

Mary broke in, overflowing with the news. "Martha is betrothed to Matthias! Can we live here with you until they marry and move into his house? We have been rejected by the disciples in Bethany. They don't admit any women now. So we want to teach here with you. Can we?"

Magdalena enfolded Mary in her arms. "There is nothing I would welcome more. Sisters, you are home now. Come in and join your family." Martha embraced Magdalena. "Congratulations, Martha. Matthias has a house in Capernaum, doesn't he? We will be near neighbors."

"Yes. He is there now, but he plans to come listen to you teach tomorrow. He also has some news to give you, not good news, I'm afraid."

"It seems that any news is bad news these days, except your arrival here today. I am so glad to have you here with us. Zeno," she called, "look who's here."

On the first night of New Moon School, most of the women arrived tired. Silent prayer and supper filled the evening, and they retired to sleep early. In the morning after breakfast and silent prayer, other women and some men arrived, including Matthias, Levi, and two men Magdalena didn't know. Zeno looked them over suspiciously and kept his eye on them. After everyone was seated in a circle in the courtyard, Magdalena spoke openly to Matthias.

"Brother Matthias, I hear you have some news to share with us."

"Yes. Just as the master expected, groups of his followers are making up their own rules about how to preach the good news and how to organize the disciples. He warned us that making too many rules would become a trap, and he was right. Down in Judea, groups are shutting others out and devising entrance codes. I am angry and frustrated."

"What sorts of rules?"

"Jewish rules: you must obey the dietary laws, the purity laws, the sabbath laws, the circumcision laws. And if you don't, you can't follow Yeshua."

Mary of Bethany chimed in, "And the men around Bethany have an all-male group that won't let any women in. Even the married men have to exclude their wives. They will let in non-Jewish, uncircumcised men, but no women."

Matthias continued, "Yes, there's that group, and there's a group that's very militant, made up of zealots, led by Barabbas. They are really an army of insurgents, but they appeal to the name of Yeshua as messiah. Barabbas even claims to be acting on Yeshua's behalf, to overthrow the Romans."

"Barabbas! The master never taught war or violence. He asked us to love enemies as if they were ourselves. How can anyone believe Barabbas speaks for him?" Magdalena said.

"Then there are the sufferers. They claim that to honor the master, we need to suffer like he did. They carry wooden crosses over their shoulders and beat themselves with whips. Roaming around the streets in gloom, they hope to anger the authorities enough to arrest them. Their highest hope is to be crucified like the master. To be martyrs."

Magdalena shook her head. "Everything Yeshua said was to help us live a full life in this world, not to make our lives miserable and seek death. Yearning for death is one of the demons the master taught us to drive out. Look around you. God's will is life. Full life in this world and a return to God for life everlasting. Life, not death. Never seek death."

Around the courtyard, the women nodded. Maybe because women had the power to bring forth life from their bodies and knew the suffering it entailed, they took life very seriously. It was not a thing to be risked lightly or thrown away carelessly. God created life and meant it to go on.

One of the new men spoke up. "What do you say about Yeshua being God? There are some followers who say he is one being with God."

Magdalena hesitated. She sensed that the stranger was testing her, and that her answer could seal her fate.

"The master never said in my hearing that he was God. He relied on God for strength and connected with God through prayer every day. Healing energy came to him from God, and to me that means that they are two separate beings. He was a man filled with love and wisdom who had reached the highest level a human can reach: being single-hearted, whole, complete. That is what I know and what we teach in this school. We try to imitate him and follow his teachings."

"So you do not worship him?" the stranger said.

"No, we worship only God. We follow Yeshua's example," Magdalena said. The man took her answer and seemed to relegate her to a category that satisfied his needs. Her group saw Yeshua as a teacher, leader, prophet, and model, but not as God. Yes, she had sealed her fate as far as this seeker was concerned.

Then Levi spoke. "Down south, there is a lot of debate going on about the death and rising of the master. The arguments grow quite heated, and groups have split up over it."

"Really? What are they saying?"

"The Jews are to blame. The Romans are to blame. God is to blame. We are to blame," Levi said.

"Wait. How is God to blame?" Magdalena asked.

"God is so angry at us sinners that he demanded a blood sacrifice of Yeshua, the perfect, unblemished human."

Magdalena's eyes widened in amazement and filled with tears. She shook her head in disbelief that such ideas were spreading around among the disciples. She took a deep breath.

"Let's stop a minute right now," she said. "We need to pray. All of us. God Almighty, we calm ourselves now and sit patiently for you to speak truth to us. Let us listen for the voice of God who loves and cares for all of us equally." Silence descended on the courtyard, and everyone prayed in her or his heart, even the new men who hadn't been taught the method Magdalena had learned from her husband.

When time had passed, Magdalena broke the silence by reciting one of the psalms she knew by heart, one of those in which King David thanked God for bringing peace out of confusion and turmoil.

"If you sensed the voice of God speaking any message to you, please share it with us. We yearn to know the truth of God's purposes," Magdalena invited. Silent hesitation held sway for several heartbeats, then Mary of Bethany spoke.

"I sensed no words, just a repudiation of the idea God is angry with us. I felt a flood of love."

"I saw light shining through clouds."

"I heard God say, 'Fear not.'"

"Did anyone see blood, violence, or killing?" Magdalena asked. No one spoke.

The new man raised an objection. "How can you know the voice or the sense you are receiving comes from God? Couldn't it just be your imagination, or Satan, or indigestion? That is no way to know about God. Only the scriptures can tell about God, and a rabbi can explain them to you. You can't talk to God through silence. That's absurd."

"See?" Levi said. "This is the kind of thing that's happening all over. If you think you can hear God through silence, you are in one camp, and if you think it's absurd, you are in another. The master wanted us to be whole, united, not all splintered like this."

"Perhaps," Magdalena said, "but if we force unity, we will have to ignore some voices. That will be a false uniformity, not the truth. I would rather have ongoing debate than oppression. The Romans are good at silencing people. So are the Sadducees. We don't want to imitate them. We want to imitate Yeshua. He listened to all sorts of people: beggars, lepers, women, Romans, Canaanites. Maybe we should too. No silencing of voices. Just listening."

"But what about those who have no learned voices to listen to? Not everyone can reach Magdala to listen to you, or Jerusalem to listen to Peter. We need to write down everything that Yeshua said to us when he was alive. Then it will be preserved as he truly said it," Matthias said.

Faces searched faces around the circle as if to ask, "Can you write?" Not many were literate. Levi, Magdalena, and Eunice were the only ones in the present group.

Eunice spoke up. "I can be your scribe, if you want to dictate to me. After it's written down once, my students are improving in their copying. If it's in Greek, that is."

"Thank you, Eunice. And thank you, all, who gave us your visions and your thoughts. I believe Zeno has our midday meal ready for us. Let's go to the kitchen."

Women and men ate together and continued to discuss the controversies surrounding the death and rising of Yeshua. The two new men slipped out quietly and never returned. They had found out what they wanted to know. Magdalena wondered whose ear they would pour their intelligence into, but she refused to worry about it. She had heard her own message during prayer, and it was one of comfort.

New Moon School met over the next two months, but after the followers left the last meeting, Mother Mary and Mary of Bethany approached Magdalena with serious faces.

"Daughter," Mother Mary said, "the men don't notice these things, but the women are talking about your condition. People will see that you are with child, and we want to protect you and the baby. We think you should go into seclusion."

"Where?"

"On the coast," Mary said. "Matthias was down in Jerusalem and talked to Joseph. He has a house in Caesarea you can use."

"And I will go with you," Mother Mary said, "to help you with my grandchild."

A picture flashed on Magdalena's inward eye: Mother Mary nine months pregnant with baby Yeshua, riding into Bethlehem on a donkey to the census. How similar would be her journey to Caesarea, riding on a donkey with Yeshua's child in her womb. She smiled at the troubled women.

"Yes, you are right. It is a good plan. When should we leave?"

"Oh, thank you, daughter, for seeing sense. We should leave soon, for the donkey's sake," and she looked pointedly at Magdalena's belly. The women laughed.

Since Magdalena had sold much of her property to finance the followers, she had little regret over leaving her house. She packed clothes and needs for the road. She would miss her women friends and other neighbors in Magdala and Capernaum. Martha and Mary would stay in the Magdala house until Martha married Matthias, calling the meetings of the school once a month. After that, Mary could live there. The master had always stressed the importance of letting go of things, and when sadness over leaving made her want to cry, she let it float up to the unseen hand. Sometimes now the hand resembled Yeshua's. The day before departure, Zeno was grooming the donkeys before putting on their packs for the journey, and two old friends appeared. Zeno called into the house.

"My lady, come see who is here. Joseph and Nicodemus."

"What! It can't be." Magdalena hurried to the door and embraced the two men. Nicodemus fell to his knees before her and bowed his head.

"Nicodemus, what's wrong?"

"Forgive me. I felt the child against me when I held you, and I realized how holy it is. I had to revere it, him, her...." The startled man began to splutter.

Magdalena lifted him by his elbow and smiled on him. "Dear Nicodemus. I am not sure about holy, but very precious. Don't apologize, just come in, cool your feet, and let us bring you refreshment. You both will stay the night, I hope."

"We plan to accompany you on the journey to Caesarea. Joseph wants to help you settle into his house and show us all the sights. I hear it's the most beautiful city in Judea. What a treat it will be to see it with you and the master's mother." Just then Mother Mary entered, catching the last of the conversation.

"How reassuring to have you with us. Welcome, Nicodemus. Welcome, Joseph."

"What is the latest news you have heard from the

south? Do you keep up with the other disciples?" Joseph asked.

"Only when Matthias or Levi brings us a report. What is happening?"

"Apparently, some spies reported to Peter about you and your school. You know what a temper he has. He takes every chance to discredit you. He is teaching a Yeshua-is-God story, complete with plenty of guilt and sin. He's organized a hierarchy in his group. He's calling himself an apostle, then there are bishops, pastors, and deacons. He loves the power of being at the top, and he wants to wipe out any remnants of you. He tells the story of your wedding on Mount Tabor very differently, and he says he was the first to see the risen master. If he finds out you are bearing the master's child, you will be in terrible danger. So we have to keep you hidden, change your name, make you disappear."

"Come now, Joseph, you are frightening her. We will do what we can, but God's protection will keep her and the baby safe. Where's your faith?" Mother Mary said.

"I bow to your wisdom. We will keep calm and do our best," Joseph said, subsiding.

"Very good. Thank you, gentlemen. Now, shall we eat? We have Martha and Zeno in the kitchen. It's bound to be delicious."

After supper, they discussed the route they would take to Caesarea.

"I think it best to take no cart. We will be less conspicuous, and if the roads are bad, we won't get stuck," Nicodemus advised.

"The best choice would be to travel south to Tiberias and then on the main road to Caesarea," Joseph added. "Three donkeys should be enough to carry two ladies and our baggage."

"We don't have a lot of possessions anyway."

"You won't need them. My house is furnished with all the bedding, pots, dishes, and furniture you will want," Joseph said. "I think you will be comfortable there. And wait till you see the sunsets from the roof. Spectacular."

Sunsets in Magdala dropped behind the hills. Magdalena had never seen a sunset over a sea.

"Let's retire. We need a good rest for our journey." And the friends bid each other good sleep.

Almost every night, Magdalena dreamed of Yeshua, and often he told her something specific she remembered clearly in the morning. She yearned for these encounters when she slept; they proved that he was right when he said love is stronger than death. On the night before the trip to Caesarea, he appeared holding a long woven stole, heavier than the usual veil she wore. He approached her, smiled warmly, and wrapped her all around in the drab colored stole, touching her on the belly when he finished. She felt a warm blessing pass into her womb from his hand. On the road to Caesarea the next day, she pondered the meaning of the dream. Plainly, he meant to protect her and the baby, but what did the weight and color of the stole mean?

Chapter 12

Caesarea

As they crested the rise surrounding the port city of Caesarea, Magdalena saw a glittering panorama open before her. Her first view of the Mediterranean caused her to take in a breath. She had lived her life by the Galilee, and she loved the blue of the water when the sky was unclouded. But she had never seen so much deep, rich blue. The sea spread as far as she could see, to the horizon. Looking at it cheered her, but her fear made her think of dreams in which she had ventured across the sea in leaky boats and been attacked by sea monsters. She preferred staying on land. Their little party of travelers stopped to appreciate the view below.

Sparkling in white stone, the Roman city of Caesarea could have been built by angels. Pillared buildings as large as the temple in Jerusalem, a splendid theater of concentric rings of seats, a huge oval hippodrome for racing horses and chariots, and the double arms of the breakwaters, embracing the harbor, dazzled the eye. At the docks, large sailing ships lined up to unload their cargoes and take on new ones. The dockside bustled with carts and people, sailors and merchants.

"There she is, the most glorious city in Palestine," Joseph said. "How do you like it?"

"Wonderful!" Mary said.

"It rivals Byzantium," Zeno said.

"And we are to live here. We are so grateful, Joseph," Magdalena said softly. "Will we be the only Jews or followers of Yeshua?"

"The city is about half Romans and half Jews. I am sure there are followers in the city, but they are keeping hidden. I suggest you not seek them out. If they mention you to the other disciples, your safety will be compromised."

"Yes, I intend to keep to myself, playing the role of a simple Jewish wife about to deliver my firstborn."

"Have you chosen your new name?"

"I will call myself 'Jael,' and Zeno I will call 'Jesse.' Mary will stay Mary; it's a common enough name. Zeno says he doesn't mind playing my husband when we go out to market or to take a stroll, but we will not attend plays or events. No use risking being seen. I will keep well-veiled in public."

"Good," Joseph said. "I will be telling the neighbors that you are my poor relations: Mary my widowed sister, you my niece, and Jesse my nephew-in-law. Will you be looking for work or should I give you an allowance? I would be happy to."

Zeno answered, "I will be looking for some kind of dock work. I am able-bodied, and I can keep an ear open to the news among the sailors and stevedores. And if Jael has any cravings, there should be exotic dainties coming in on the ships. I think we will live comfortably. We can't thank you enough."

"I have some money with me, and I can take in copy work or write letters for women," Magdalena added. "There aren't very many female scribes, and most ladies would rather not dictate personal letters to a man. I still have months to wait until I have a baby to care for."

Mother Mary asked, "Joseph, where in this huge city is your house?"

"It's not far from the docks, in a modest street of mostly Jewish households. You will be safe and inconspicuous there. Let me lead the way."

Joseph strode on ahead. Zeno led Sophia carrying Jael, smiling at the name Magdalena had chosen for herself, the former name of her donkey. Nicodemus led the donkey carrying Mother Mary, and the pack animal trailed behind on a lead. Down the broad and clean streets they descended, following Joseph past the temple of Mithras, the open market, and one of the synagogues the city boasted. Roman guards encircled the high-perched palace of Pontius Pilate, who ruled from Caesarea most of the time, traveling to Jerusalem only when necessary. Magdalena didn't blame him for staying by the beautiful seaside, only for condemning her husband to death.

Joseph's house had a door opening onto the street and a central courtyard. A well stocked kitchen, three sleeping rooms, and a staircase to the roof assured the new tenants they could live well there. Zeno put his small bundle into the smallest room, the two women took one of the large rooms, and the two men took the other. Tired from their long journey, the travelers rested. Tomorrow they would view the sights.

The next day a hollow fear took over Magdalena's

will, and she asked to be excused from the sightseeing. Mother Mary wanted to rest another day, also, so the three men set off alone. Nicodemus and Zeno had never been to Caesarea. Nicodemus wanted to see the palace and the hippodrome. If they were lucky, perhaps a race would be in progress. They could afford a ticket, but they could also see the action from the rise above the town. Zeno hoped to investigate the docks and the possibilities of work.

"Daughter, are you afraid to go out?" Mother Mary asked after the men left.

"Yes, maybe I will stay inside the entire time we are here."

"At least you have to see the sunset from the roof."

Magdalena smiled and took the opportunity to climb the steps to the roof. The grade of the city lifted the house just enough above the neighboring houses that she had a view of the water beyond the docks. Two stools were already on the roof, so she sat on one and watched until the low sun touched the horizon. A golden path of light led from the sun to her, beckoning her toward the west. She felt Yeshua's hand reaching out to her also as part of that golden configuration. When the sun sank, the sky turned orange, pink and purple in a shading gradient so beautiful she took in her breath. With that breath she breathed in peace, and she knew God and Yeshua were watching over her. It would be all right. She told herself she needn't fear.

The next day, Nicodemus and Joseph left, taking two of the three donkeys. Joseph promised to return when he could, to check on them and bring news from Jerusalem. Nicodemus also hoped to see the baby when it came, and to revisit the city he had become enamored of. Just before they set off, Joseph introduced them to their neighbors: Rachel and Eli, and their two children Susanna and John. As they parted, Rachel whispered to Magdalena.

"I've had plenty of experience delivering babies, so just send your husband over when you need me. Is this your first?"

"No, second." Magdalena felt shy at saying that, and Rachel looked confused since there obviously was no older child in the household. "She died."

Rachel took her hand and pressed it. "I am sorry. This one will thrive, God willing."

Then farewells passed from person to person, and the small family of Jael, Jesse, and Mary settled into their new home for the night.

The next day, Jesse learned that occasional laborers were always needed when a ship sat at the dock, either to unload cargo or lay new cargo in the hold for export. If no ships were in, there was no work. His daily routine became an early morning walk to the docks to ask about work followed by a full day of hard labor on the ships or a walk back home to spend the day with the two women. He did odd jobs around the house or housework the women let him do. He happily went to market and cooked meals, especially after he started earning wages and could buy novel items from the cargoes that came in from Greece, Rome, and Spain. One day he brought some wine imported from Gaul. All of them drank it and became quite animated. Laughter filled the house. The next day, Jael didn't feel well, so she gave up wine for the rest of her pregnancy, though she admitted it was the finest wine she had tasted since Eunice and Jude's wedding.

Jael learned that the Romans regulated and taxed the work of scribes. Not wanting to tangle with governmental agents, she used word of mouth to advertise her skills to the neighbors secretly. She told Rachel that she was available to write ladies' letters in Greek or Aramaic for a small fee, with no tax added. Word of her freelance writing service spread slowly, quietly, among her Jewish neighbors. Nobody wanted to tip the Romans off and make trouble for Jael. She wrote one or two letters every few days and earned enough for ink and papyrus, plus a bit extra for baby things. Meeting the women in the neighborhood without having to go out was another benefit of her business. She heard all the latest gossip and met some friendly women willing to tell her about the best midwives, vendors, and apothecaries. Mother Mary also enjoyed sitting in on these conversations, often serving tea and small cakes she had baked. The Jesse household became popular over the months.

Jael knew her days were nearing their end when the baby's position dropped lower. One night she dreamed that she woke up to see Yeshua standing over her. He said clearly, "No midwife." Just after he said that, a sharp labor pain racked her body and she cried out. Mary, lying near her woke and came to her side.

"Is it starting, Daughter? Shall I send Jesse for Rachel?"

"No, Yeshua told me not to employ a midwife." Mary didn't question her. She knew about Jael's many visions and dreams. They had all come true, one way or another. Another pain struck.

"I feel the need to push," Jael said.

"Surely not yet," Mary said.

But Jael's body had a mind of its own, and she pushed. The baby emerged in one smooth motion and landed in Mary's gentle hands. Her eyes widened. She had never seen such a thing, though she had heard of it. The baby slept curled up in a ball, entirely encased in the birth sac. No water, no blood, no tearing, but also no breath. Mary tore a hole in the sac over the baby's nose, and a breath and a cry emerged. Then she slipped the membrane off the baby carefully, releasing the water also.

"It's a girl child," Mary said.

Jesse came running with the knife he had sharpened the day before and some strong string to tie off the cord.

"I know why Yeshua told you not to use a midwife. There's no way you could keep the baby's being born in the full sac a secret. That would call too many people's attention," Mary said.

"It's good luck," Jesse said. "She will be a witch, or a healer, or a prophet."

Jael smiled, thinking to herself that Jesse was probably right, with her parentage.

"I will name her Eroica," Jael said.

"A good name for a brave, strong woman," Mary said, smiling at the wet baby in her hands. Wrapping the infant in a cloth, she handed her to her mother. In the semi-darkness, Jael saw a faint green glow circling the child's head. She wondered if Yeshua had that halo at birth, but she refrained from asking Mary. The infant opened her eyes and looked directly at her mother with a cognizance not known in newborns. Then she burrowed for the teat and began to suckle. Jael thanked God for the easiest birth known to womankind, and let her milk flow.

Jesse asked, "What shall I do with the sac? It's a good luck charm. I'll lay it out to dry."

"It will stick to whatever you lay it on. Put it on a sheet of Jael's papyrus to dry."

"Then I will make Eroica a little amulet to keep it in, for protection," Jesse said.

Jael smiled at her devoted friend. "Yes, if you wish. She will need all the protection we can give her."

The letter Jael wrote a few days after the birth brought Joseph and Nicodemus back to Caesarea. They wanted to see the child of Yeshua with as much ardor as they would have wanted to see Yeshua himself. They took turns holding Eroica and exclaiming on her bright eyes and strong grip.

"Hello, Eroica, I am your great-granduncle, Joseph." Jael smiled but paid little heed until Joseph turned to her and asked, "Did you know that?"

Jael was startled. "What do you mean? I thought we were only pretending you are our uncle."

"No, I actually am Mary's uncle. Her father was my brother, so that makes me Eroica's great-granduncle."

"Oh, how wonderful! So you were Yeshua's granduncle. No wonder you wanted to collect his body."

"Yes, that was one reason."

"When Joseph, my husband, died, Yeshua was only 12 years old, so Uncle Joseph became like a father to him," Mary explained.

"Oh, tell me all about how he was as a boy. I never knew any of this."

Jesse and Nicodemus also leaned in to hear the tales of Yeshua's boyhood.

"Well, the death of his father knocked the wind out of him, and I thought it would be good to get him out of Nazareth for a while. At the time, I was trading in tin for the Romans, and they were about to send me to manage the mines in Britannia. I thought Yeshua might take his mind off his loss if he went on a big adventure, and there was a famous wisdom school there, taught by Druids where he could learn more of God. So, he shipped out with me on a tin trader, and we went to Britannia."

"How long were you there?" Jesse asked.

"I had signed a sixteen year contract, but I knew if Yeshua grew homesick for his family, I could send him home on any ship bringing tin to Palestine. He stayed with me the full sixteen years. He loved the greenness of the place. It rains there all the time, and there are lush trees and fields as far as you can see. It's nothing like Palestine. And he excelled in the school."

"What did he do all day while you worked?"

"First, he built us a little house using the local materials and methods, very different from the stone work he learned from his father. He wove a basket-like structure of little tree trunks and plastered it over with something called 'daub.' Then he made a roof of the reeds that grow in the marshes all over. That was tricky. He had lessons from a local man. The first rain came right through and we got soaked. Next day, he started over again. That one held the whole time we lived there. Once he entered the Druid university, he spent the day memorizing his lessons. Some were taught in Greek, which he knew, but he had no trouble learning the British tongue they spoke in that region. Even at that young age, he impressed his tutors."

"How did you worship God?" Jael asked.

"Of course, Yeshua learned about God all day, the version of God the Druids teach. We prayed to Yahweh and argued scripture alone in our house at night. There were no other Jews that we knew about. He became a sharp thinker when anything about God was up for discussion. I tried to ask him hard questions, just to make him struggle. He always convinced me he was right."

"What about the sabbath?"

"The Romans work every day, so I did too. They are lenient about Jews here in Palestine taking the day off, but not in Britannia. Yeshua said the prayers and made a sabbath meal of sorts for me when I came home from work. I always thought those years loosened him up about keeping the sabbath, and that's why he got in trouble with the priests. I feel guilty if I corrupted him over there."

Jael smiled. "Don't blame yourself, Uncle. Yeshua had his own ideas. I wonder, did he try healing people when he was young?"

"He would take long walks through the woods and marshes, collecting flowers, seeds, and roots. He took them to the women Druids for instruction. At first, they had trouble talking, but they taught him what was poisonous, what was good for pain, what could heal a wound, and things like that. Most of the women Druids learn the healing arts. The priestly Druids are mostly men. Then there is a class of artist Druids of both sexes who make songs and poems. Yeshua studied under the priestly Druid tutors."

"But I never saw him use herbs to heal," Nicodemus said.

"No, but it taught him that God has sealed up healing into all of creation. Every creature can heal itself from within."

"Is that what he meant when he said 'your faith has healed you'?" Jesse asked.

"Maybe. He was convinced that God has given us all we need already, and it is inside us, now."

Jael had gone quiet, remembering her husband's voice uttering those words.

Joseph resumed, "Another practice he learned there

was praying silently under a tree. There were so many beautiful trees to choose from: oak, ash, elm, and maple. He prayed under all of them. He also sat under fruit trees like crab apple, cherry and pear. When he chose those, we usually had a treat for supper." Everyone laughed. "The Druids prefer the oak tree, which they deem holy."

"He always chose an olive tree here," Mary said.

"I think he felt anointed by the tree. At least that's what I feel," Jael said.

"Well, there are no olive trees over there. It's too cold. Which reminds me, I did catch him one time lighting a fire with his powers. We always had a fire in our hut at night for warmth, and Yeshua was excellent at laying the wood just so to burn all night. That night he had misplaced the flint fire-starter we used, and he just started it himself. I shook my finger at him and acted offended. He was a boy. What boy would not want to use his powers? I was always amazed at the self-control he had."

"Yes, I had to speak to him about magical performances when he was about seven or eight," Mary said, wistfully.

"Why did you think it necessary to stifle him?" Jael asked, thinking about raising Eroica if she had such powers.

"Mostly it was to protect him. We didn't want him to show off, draw attention, make trouble," Mary said.

"Lighting a fire in his own hearth at home couldn't draw attention," Jael said.

"No, but I was just in the habit of correcting him. I learned it from Mary," Joseph said.

"It's not easy raising a special child. I always second guessed myself. After Yeshua, his brothers and sisters were easy."

Jesse asked, "Do you think Eroica will be special?"

Jael looked down into the face of her sleeping daughter, "I am afraid so."

———————— • • ————————

By the end of her first year, Eroica was walking and talking. Often, her mother found her chatting away to no one. At first, Jael assumed she was babbling to an invisible friend, but she soon realized that Yeshua was her interlocutor. Eroica would ask a question then listen for the answer. Sometimes she would laugh at what she heard in her mind's ear. Then she would talk some more. Jael never interrupted these talks. If her daughter could have her father with her, even through mystical communication, she was glad. As Eroica's speech improved, sometimes Jael could understand the gist of the conversation. Eroica often asked Yeshua if he was well, happy, hungry, lonely, or sad. Once she saw Eroica mime embracing her father, and Jael's eyes filled with tears. She was raising a special child.

As soon as the girl could sit still, she joined the adults in silent prayer. Their city house had no nearby tree, so they prayed in the courtyard, or sometimes on the roof. This new channel to the divine enhanced Eroica's conversations with her father Yeshua. She no longer had to speak to him in words. She remained in his presence all day and night, sometimes smiling or laughing for no apparent reason. None of the family tried to stifle her. Had she been out in the public eye, her behavior might have elicited speculation about her sanity. More likely, people would say she was possessed by a demon. But Jael knew, as did Jesse and Mary, that Eroica was possessed by God's love and thrived on it.

When Jesse didn't have work at the dock, he often took Eroica out to explore the city. By age three she had walked or been carried all over Caesarea. She had shopped in the market, watched men fishing at the shore, observed the changing of the guard at the palace, and stood on the rise to watch a chariot race at the hippodrome. That day, she became agitated when she saw the charioteers whipping their horses to run faster.

"Papa, the horses don't like that."

"How do you know?" Jesse asked.

"They told me. It hurts."

When Jael heard this report, she reassured Eroica that she would not have to watch any more races.

"They should stop," Eroica said. "Men shouldn't hurt horses. Or any animals."

"That's true. But we do eat some animals for food."

"Why?"

Jael hesitated. She looked at Jesse, then at Mary.

Mary spoke. "God says we can eat some animals for food."

Eroica seemed to accept whatever God said, but she added, "Those men were not eating. They hit the horses for fun." No one could argue with her. Racing was for fun, and gambling, and greed. As Jael thought more about it, Eroica was announcing something profound. She was her father's child.

———————• •———————

One day when Eroica was about four years old, Jesse asked Jael if he could take her down to the docks. Jael, of course, hesitated. She still clung to her old fear of the sea.

"I will be with her all the time," Jesse said, "and I will

make sure she wears her amulet."

Jael looked over at Mary, seeking advice. Mary nodded.

"All right, but be watchful."

"I will. There is a beautiful Chinese trader docked, and I think she will like it. We will be back soon." Eroica had retrieved her good luck amulet and was wearing it, jumping up and down at the door. "Come, little one," Jesse said, taking her hand, "let's have an adventure."

After they left, Mary said, "You can't protect her forever."

"I know. I just have this irrational fear of the water. And I have been having water nightmares a lot lately. I hope it's not an omen."

"You are the seer. You can tell better than I what is an omen. But if you are worried, you should pray about it. In fact, let me pray for you now."

"Yes, Mother," Jael said and bowed her head.

"Heavenly God, maker of the universe and all of the oceans, please free your daughter Jael from her fear of water. She is holding her fear up to you now, asking you to take it away. I pray in the name of Yeshua, your son. Amen."

After the prayer, Jael felt lighter, but of course she was sitting safe in her own home, not in a boat on the sea. Later, she would have to test the prayer's effect. For now, she smiled at Mary and said,

"Thank you, Mother; thank you, God."

The two adventurers didn't return for two hours, and Jael tried to resist the worry. The walk to the dock and back took only an hour, unless you made a detour through the market. Perhaps that's what Jesse and Eroica had done.

Before they appeared in the doorway, the child's

voice announced their arrival.

"Mama, Mama! I swam with the fishes! I touched an otter!"

Jesse entered sheepishly, holding the dripping girl wrapped in his outer robe. Her hair was tangled and wet, but her face glowed with excitement.

"What happened?" Jael said as her daughter ran into her arms when Jesse released her from her wrap.

"I talked to some fish. Then I went in to pick a red star from the post. I sank in the water. It was dark and funny. Then a mama otter lifted me up, and Papa pulled me out. I want to go back!"

Jael embraced the girl, trembling.

"Don't be scared, Mama. I wasn't scared. I liked it. The sea animals talk to me. I love them."

Jael looked at Jesse, who shrugged. "It's true. She wasn't interested in the ship when there were fish to talk to. I don't know if the amulet saved her or the otter. She was not afraid at all."

"Mama, I want to go back. I want to swim every day. Please?"

"I don't know. The dock is a dangerous place."

"I could take her to the strand along the bay. The water's shallow and the waves very small. It would be a good place to learn," Jesse suggested.

"Do you know how to swim?"

"Enough," Jesse said.

"I know how. I know how," Eroica bubbled. "Please, Mama."

"All right. But for now, bring a comb and let me untangle that mop of hair."

"Hooray! Thank you, Mama. Thanks, Papa. I will swim with my friends!" and she scurried off to find the comb.

After that, Eroica swam any day that Jesse could take

her to the bay for practice. If he had to work, she stood on the roof and looked out to sea. From there she saw families of dolphins leaping above the waves and whales spouting as they came up for air. She spoke to all of them and heard them speak back. When Jael questioned her about what the whales said, Eroica usually replied, "They love me. They love the sea. They love each other. They love God." Always love was their message, and Jael knew her daughter was telling the truth as she heard it. Love was the truth, whether it came from a whale, a human, or God in heaven.

On the roof, Eroica also met with the birds. Sea gulls would come to her and take bread from her hand, if she sneaked some from the kitchen for them. They told her the same story the whales told. A sparrow built a nest in the corner of the roof wall, and Eroica watched the construction with wonder, sitting very still on the stool. When baby sparrows hatched in the nest, her joy was uncontainable. She had to drag all her family up to the roof in celebration of the new life and new love. Jael, Jesse, and Mary praised God for the gift of such a child.

But Jael's nightmares had not stopped, and Mary's grandmotherly heart sensed with foreboding that their joy couldn't last. They continued to pray.

Chapter 13

Rhodes

Jael sat alone on the roof to soak up the sunset, thanking God and Yeshua for her many blessings. The golden road of light stretched from the sinking sun toward her, and she closed her eyes. She saw her daughter Eroica in her birth sac, only she was not a newborn. She was her current age, about five. Peering through the membrane, Eroica smiled at her mother, beckoning her to join her. Instantly, Jael was inside the sac with her child. Then the sac fell into water, the dark harbor by the dock. She and Eroica floated slowly down, and the sac expanded again. Now, Mary was with them in the sac. The three laughed at their predicament. Suddenly, the membrane stretched to a huge size, and a whole sailing ship was within it. Jael saw that Jesse and Joseph were standing on the deck, looking in the direction of the setting sun. The ship sailed west borne by a pleasant wind, fearless within its protective sac, along the golden road. When she opened her eyes, she knew that the vision was true and intended to reassure her that all would be well. Her entire family was safe, protected, and bound for something good. She consciously locked this vision in her memory, for she knew she would need it to strengthen her.

The next day, a sweaty young messenger arrived with a short letter from Joseph. It said, "Coming to visit. Leaving Monday. Joseph."

Jael read the letter to Jesse and Mary.

"Why so short? How long is he staying? Is he bringing Nicodemus?" Mary asked.

"He's in a hurry, and he didn't want to give much away. He's afraid of spies," Jesse said.

Eroica piped up, "He shouldn't be afraid. We will keep Uncle safe. I can show him my bird's nest and how I can swim!"

"Yes, you can. Would you like to help? You can fetch the broom and sweep Uncle's room before he comes."

"Yes, I will," and she skipped to the kitchen for the broom. While the child was out of the courtyard, Jesse continued.

"I think we should pack up some necessities. If Joseph is coming in a hurry, he may want us to leave here. Someone has told about Eroica in Jerusalem. She is not safe. I will sharpen my short sword and dagger."

Mary and Jael shared a worried look. Swords and daggers? Surely those would not be needed. But they packed up some clothes and food for a journey, just in case.

When Joseph arrived, early Tuesday morning after journeying by moonlight, they learned how right Jesse had been. Joseph collapsed onto a cushion, drank some of the water Mary brought, and told his news.

"Someone from Caesarea told Peter that you had come here after leaving Magdala. At first, he wasn't concerned, as long as you were out of his way so he could slander you and edit Yeshua's teachings to suit his needs. Then he heard that a child was seen coming and going from your house. Fearing that it was Yeshua's child and that she might be able to attract disciples of her own on that account, he hired Simon the Zealot and Barabbas to come here to kill her, and Jael as well, if they can. They will not set out until after the sabbath, so we have a few days."

"We've already packed," Jesse said.

"Good. What about weapons?"

"I've sharpened my two blades. I will prepare yours as well."

"Thank you," Joseph said, handing over his sword. "I hope it will not come to that. I have an escape plan. There's a ship at the dock, the *Argenti*."

"Yes, I have been loading it this week. It sails in two days, or whenever the wind is favorable."

"It is headed west. I want us all to be on it. They will take passengers, and if I pay them enough they will keep their mouths shut," Joseph said.

Here was the first test of Jael's sea fear, the idea of traveling by ship. She summoned the vision of the protective membrane and the pleasant feeling it evoked. Taking a deep breath, she let go of her tension and didn't protest Joseph's plan. Neither did Mary. Eroica jumped with joy.

"We will sail in a big ship! Uncle Joseph, you are my hero. When do we leave?"

"That all depends on the wind," Joseph said. "Pray for a wind to blow us west and north."

"Oh, yes, I will," she said, and scurried to the roof to

pray to God over her beloved sea.

In the room below, Jael asked, "Where are we headed?"

"The first port of call is Rhodes. Then along the coast going west to Gaul. Then we will take a river route across Gaul to the northern sea and across to Britannia. If God is with us. Have you had any favorable dreams or visions, Jael?"

"Yes, I have. Visions of protection over ship travel."

"Praise God. We will hold fast to that so we don't lose our nerve," Joseph said.

"Yeshua will fight by our side," Jesse said. Jael wasn't so sure about that, but said nothing. "After you rest, Joseph, do you want to walk down to the dock to see our vessel?"

"I think not. I don't want to be seen until we depart. But take this purse down to the captain of the *Argenti*, and see if he will book us five places, and swear him to secrecy. If no cabins are available, we will take whatever accommodation he has. Use all the money if you have to."

Jesse took the purse, his dagger, and went to the dock on a mission.

The next day, the voice of their neighbor Eli came through the door. "Is Joseph here? Or Jesse?"

"I am here," Joseph said, "What has happened?" Jesse entered right behind him.

"Two of Pilate's guards were found behind the palace with their throats cut. Their uniforms were missing," Eli said.

"Then the assassins will be disguised as Roman guards. We must go---now!" Joseph said, grabbing some of the packed bundles.

"Eroica, grab your bag. And your amulet," Jael said. She knew it was superstitious to think the amulet would save them, but she grasped at every straw while simultaneously praying to God.

Carrying their packs, they hurried to the dock and approached the ship. The captain recognized Jesse and gestured them aboard. As they climbed the gangplank, Eroica turned her head and saw two Roman soldiers in armor and red uniforms approaching. They both wore swords on their sides. At the same time she looked at a skiff tied to the dock, and she acted.

"Mama, Grandmary, follow me." She took Jael and Mary by the hands and pulled them down the plank, along the wharf, and down the steps to a floating dock below. Marshaling the older women into the small boat, she bid them lie down and pulled a tarp over them. The three lay side by side and waited in silence. Jael felt like baby Moses in the bulrushes, only she was as frightened as Moses' mother. From their muffled hiding place, they heard the heavy steps of the soldiers and clanking of their armor as they boarded the ship.

"We need to see all your passengers," the soldier said.

A voice answered, "Yes, of course. Who are you looking for?" Jael assumed that was the captain's voice.

"A Jewess and a little girl."

"Ha! Well, I assure you we have no women or girls on board, though it might be pleasant to have some. Ha! Search all you want." And Jael heard the soldiers' heavy tramp move away to search the ship. She held Eroica's hand on one side and Mary's on the other. All three prayed without ceasing.

As they waited for the men to search, they felt a bump against the prow of the skiff, then another. Silently and smoothly the boat started moving. They didn't dare call out in case the soldiers heard them. Maybe it was Jesse, swimming in the water and pulling them. They lay silent. The movement continued, and the sounds of the busy dock faded. Under the tarp, all they could hear was the lapping of water against the sides of the boat. Then another sound came: the shrill chirp of a dolphin.

"My friends are here!" Eroica said, under her breath. "Let me thank them for saving us," and she sat up, pulling the tarp back so she could see her friends.

When Mary and Jael looked back, Caesarea was far off in the distance. They could see the *Argenti* still waiting at the dock, but they could not see Joseph or Jesse. Eroica continued to chatter to the dolphins, now six or eight of them gathered all around the boat. Eroica pulled the loose end of the rope out of the water.

"Mama, we need to tie a loop in this rope to make it easier for the dolphins."

Wide-eyed, Jael took it and did her best to tie a knot in the swollen rope, leaving a loop about the size of a dolphin's snout.

"They are going to take turns pulling us. They get tired. We are heavy." Eroica tossed the rope into the water, and one of the dolphins put his nose through the loop and began swimming.

"Where are they taking us?"

"Didn't Uncle Joseph say Rhodes? That's what I told them. Rhodes." After living with her for five years, Mary and Jael were used to the girl's strange pronouncements. They had learned to believe what she said. Mary patted her granddaughter's knee and smiled on her. Jael shook her head and laughed.

The dolphins pulled the boat in shifts all night while the women tried to sleep, wrapped in their stoles. Jael remembered the dream of the long, heavy stole, and she wished for such a stole now. She had never thought about how cold it could be on the water. When the sun rose, she sat up and looked under the tarp at the other end of the boat. There she found a clay jar of water and a sack of thin, dry bread. Also, a stem of dates lay in the salty water in the boat's bottom.

"Thank you, God," she breathed. "Look, we have breakfast." And she served the feast to her mother-in-law and her daughter.

"How far is Rhodes? Maybe we should ration the food," Mary suggested.

"I have no idea," Jael said.

"Oh, no, Grandmary, we should eat it up. God will send more," Eroica said, taking another cracker to munch on. "Papa said."

"Which Papa?"

"My real Papa, the one in heaven. He said not to fear, there would be plenty."

So for the next four days, the women ate dry bread and dates and drank fresh water from the jar. Whenever they went to the sack of bread, it was full. Whenever they tipped up the jug, water flowed out. Dates sprouted on the stem wherever they had picked them.

On the last day, the dolphins sang a farewell to Eroica and her family, chattering and smiling all around the boat. Eroica petted them on their heads from the boat and thanked them.

"But we are out in the middle of the sea. If they leave us here, what will we do?" Jael lamented.

"They will hand us off to the whale. See, here he comes!" And Eroica pointed to a spout of spray arising at a short distance. The fin whale's huge head arose on Eroica's side of the boat as if to make her acquaintance.

He seemed to be smiling. Then he took the rope and pulled them through the water. His speed was about the same as the dolphins', but he was much stronger and didn't need to rest as often. As the sun was going down, he escorted the boat into the harbor at Rhodes, leaving them as close in as the shallowness of the water would allow. He didn't want to beach himself on the gravel. The whale leaped from the water and waved a fin to them as he departed. Eroica waved to him and called, "Thank you, whale. I love you."

Soon they heard voices shouting on the breakwater. The fishermen saw that the boat was stranded without sail or oars. Luckily, the tide was rolling toward the shore when a small rowboat came out to meet them and tow them in. The women thanked the men with gestures and the Greek words Jael knew, following them to their house on the waterfront where a woman named Neri gave them dinner.

"See, Mama," Eroica said, "I told you we would be safe."

"Tell us the story of how you sailed here in a boat with no sails," Neri's husband asked, tearing a piece of bread and wiping his plate with it.

Mary, as the eldest, narrated their journey honestly to their hosts. Eroica added vivid details about dolphins and whales. The listeners' eyes grew wider and wider.

"So, you are blessed people whom the gods want to keep safe. We are honored to have you under our roof. Do you intend to stay on Rhodes or travel onward?"

"We don't know. We are grateful to be alive, but our men must think we are dead. Will any ship be going to Palestine to take a letter to them?"

"Not soon," answered Neri. "The next ship should be the *Argenti*, but it will be bound west to Gaul."

"That is the ship we were supposed to board."

"When it arrives, we can ask what happened to your family. For now, you need your sleep. I will put you in our bed, through here," and Neri led them to a sleeping room.

———————— • ————————

Neri's husband woke Jael in the morning, excited.

"The *Argenti* docked in the night. Come!"

All three arose and followed him to the breakwater. There stood the *Argenti*, unloading some goods and passengers. Halfway down the gangplank walked Joseph and Jesse. Eroica broke from her mother's hand and ran.

"Papa, Papa! Here we are!" The men looked up, and the gloom on their faces departed.

"God be praised, you are alive," Jesse said, taking her in his arms. Joseph raised his hands to heaven and breathed a thanksgiving. By then the women arrived at the foot of the ramp.

"Oh, my lady, how glad I am to see you alive. We thought you had drowned. What happened to you?"

"It is a long and strange story. This is our kind host who rescued us from the sea and kept us safe over night," Jael said.

"God bless you, sir," said Joseph bowing. "I hope you will accept this payment for your hospitality." The man took the purse Joseph handed him graciously, and gestured that the men should follow him to his house.

Neri was happy to meet the father and uncle of Eroica, whom she had become fond of. She offered refreshment, and many smiles passed around the room.

"The captain has given us a large cabin we can all share, until we reach Ostia. Then a Roman official will have it, and we will sleep on the deck. We should return to the ship soon, so he knows we still intend to travel on," Joseph said.

They bid farewell to their hosts, Eroica making sure to embrace and kiss Neri. She and her husband walked them to the dock and waved good-bye.

Once on board the *Argenti,* the family retired to their cabin and shared their stories. Eroica went first since she was the most impatient. Joseph and Jesse enjoyed hearing about the friendly dolphins and whale that had pulled them to Rhodes at Eroica's request. The self-renewing food and water also struck them with its supernatural goodness. But they had their own weird tale to tell.

"The assassins searched the whole ship looking for a girl and a woman. I recognized Simon the Zealot under his visor, and he recognized me," Jesse said. "But when the other man asked if they should take us instead, Simon told him no. He said they were sent for women, not men, and they left the ship. We looked for you all over the dock but couldn't find you. We prayed. The captain saw how upset we were, and he prayed too, to his god that protects travelers. He even burned a little incense in a brazier on the deck and chanted some words in a strange tongue. As the smoke rose up, I watched it, thinking maybe it would reach God in heaven and carry our prayers. Then all three of us, Joseph, the captain, and I heard a voice and looked up. There was a white figure with wings standing in the smoke. I call it an angel, but the captain calls it a daemon. It said, 'Go to Rhodes.' It repeated it in Aramaic and Greek. Then it disappeared. We all looked at each other. We couldn't believe what we had seen, but we all saw it and heard it."

"And that is why we are here, right where God

intended us to be, all along. We just came by different means," Joseph added, smiling. Eroica threw her little arms about his neck and kissed his cheek.

"I have a question," Jesse said, "do you think we could go back to our real names now? We are far from the threat of Jerusalem, aren't we?"

"Maybe yes, maybe no, but we have the angels on our side, so I say let's not live in fear," Jael said. "From now on, please call me Magdalena, and I will call you Zeno."

"I will still call you Papa and Mama," Eroica said. "I know my real papa is in heaven, but who says a girl can't have two?"

Her family laughed and allowed that she was right. The next day, the *Argenti* set sail for Italia and the great Roman port of Ostia.

Chapter 14

Gaul

At Ostia, the family removed their meager belongings from their cabin and found an out-of-the- way corner of the top deck to stow them. An important-looking Roman in a long toga and his elegant wife boarded and moved into the large cabin. After a time, the ship set off to Massilia, the Roman port on the coast of Gaul. Eroica loved watching the passing coastline and the deep blue water. She saw a few dolphins and many sea gulls. Magdalena overheard her conversing with her Papa in heaven and exclaiming over the wonders of sailing. The family bedded down on the deck that night, and the next day arrived in sight of the walled city of Massilia with its long, sheltered harbor.

"The captain gave me directions to the river boat dock, but perhaps we should sleep at an inn for the night. I didn't sleep well on the deck," Joseph said.

"Neither did I," Zeno said.

"Let's look for an inn near the river boats." The group set off through the busy city, carrying their bundles. Zeno held Eroica's hand as she skipped along gaily.

"Look, Papa Zeno! I've never seen so many big ships! And look at all the people!"

Suddenly, they turned a corner and Magdalena's eyes fell on a small inn. A green glow surrounded the door. "That's the one," she said. The outline of a fish was painted over the door.

"Why that one?" Zeno asked.

"I just have a feeling."

"If she has a feeling, we should follow her," Joseph said. "Let's see if they have rooms for us."

A heavily pregnant woman met them in the inn's front room.

"May we have lodging for the night?" Mary asked.

"Yes, welcome," the woman said. "With supper?"

"Yes, please."

"Where are you traveling to?"

Joseph replied, "We are traveling to Britannia."

"Why? That place is cold and gray. It never stops raining. Better to stay here where we have sunshine and the best wine in the world. May I pour you some?"

"Maybe with our meal," Joseph said.

Eroica approached the woman curiously. She had never seen a pregnant woman up close.

"May I touch your baby?" she asked.

"Yes, little one, if you wish," the woman said.

Eroica put both her hands on the woman's belly, laid her mouth close by and said, "Hello, baby, I love you. God loves you, too. I hope you come out to see us before we leave. I want to kiss you."

The woman started to chuckle, but the child in her womb jerked suddenly and a gush of water dripped on the floor.

"Well," the woman said, "I was hoping this child would get on with its birth, and this magical girl has made my wish come true. Let me mop up this water."

Magdalena knew the green glow had brought her to the inn for a reason, and this was it. "I will be glad to help you, if you don't have a midwife already."

"Thank you. I feel like the gods sent you to me. My heart welcomes you." A sudden pain stopped the woman's breath.

"Let's go to your room. Do you have a birthing stool?" And the innkeeper showed the men to their room and took Magdalena, Mary and Eroica with her to the room where the birth would take place.

Zeno stuck his head into the room. "Can I bring your husband?"

"He is at the docks picking up a shipment. He will be home directly."

The woman's name was Enid. She was large and strong, able to withstand a long labor. Eroica was in her element. She sang lullabies to Enid and mopped her forehead. She brought cool drinks and small edibles to keep up the mother's strength. When the baby's head made its first appearance, Enid said Eroica could touch the child's wet scalp if she wanted to. Eroica beamed, and gently patted the baby, cooing to it and urging it to join her in the wonderful world.

"Papa," Eroica said, "take away Enid's pain, and help the baby come out. Amen."

At that moment, Enid felt the urge to push, and the baby was born. Magdalena caught the tiny boy and wiped him clean. Mary tied and cut the cord. Eroica watched in amazement. Just then, Enid's husband returned from the docks to meet his new son. He had been delayed by some mix-up with the customs agents.

"Enid! You wonderful woman. Look what you birthed, a son and heir," he said.

Magdalena put the baby in Enid's arms. Enid gave him to her husband, Bran, who handled the child well for a first-time father. The baby fit snugly into the crook of his arm. Bran showed his son proudly to Joseph and Zeno, then took him out into the front room of the inn to exhibit him to the guests who sat drinking wine and beer.

"How can I thank you all?" Enid said to the women. "I was afraid, but you all gave me courage."

"We were happy to help. Now do you have a cook to make the evening meals?"

"I usually do the cooking. There's a pot of stew on the stove, simmering. But there's no bread made."

"Zeno is very good in the kitchen. We will take care of feeding ourselves and the guests. You need to rest," Magdalena said. "Come, Eroica, let's leave Enid to sleep."

"Wait. When the girl prayed, which god did she pray to? I want to name my son for that god."

"I prayed to my Papa in heaven," Eroica said.

"Do you mean Yahweh? Are you Jews?"

"We are Jews who follow the teachings of Yeshua," Magdalena said.

Enid's eyes grew wide. "What are those teachings?"

"Enid, you must rest. We will talk in the morning," Mary said and hurried everyone out of the room.

The next day dawned rainy and blustery. Though Joseph wanted to proceed on the river, the women convinced him to wait one more day. They wanted to spend another day with Enid, sharing the good news of Yeshua's teachings, and Eroica wanted to kiss the baby more. She carried on long conversations with him, listening as much as she spoke, answering his questions about living in the physical world: the sun, the moon, the day and night, food, water, play, walking, learning, love, and God. She delighted in answering whatever she heard him ask, and Magdalena delighted in hearing her answers. Was it her fertile imagination, or did she really communicate with the baby who as yet had no language? Magdalena didn't judge. She let Eroica be who she was. The baby seemed to respond to the attention with peace and small movements of his mouth and limbs.

Enid and Bran knew about the God of the Jews, though they were Gauls who still worshiped the old gods. As innkeepers, they spoke with many travelers and enjoyed hearing about their views on the divine. A few secret followers of Yeshua might have passed through their inn, but they weren't sure, and after such visitors disappeared into the city, they never saw them again.

"Your God is a god of love, but powerful to protect, too. I want to know more of this god."

"We have to be going tomorrow," Joseph warned, unless Magdalena should stay longer.

"Can you read Greek?" Magdalena asked.

"A little, but our neighbor does. We trust him," Bran said.

"I will write to you more of Yeshua's teachings," Magdalena said. "How should I direct it?"

"To Bran, or Enid, Sign of the Salmon, Massilia. That should reach us."

Enid spoke up. "I want to name our son Esus. It's a Gaulish name, but it will remind us of your prophet."

Eroica jumped for joy. "Esus, oh how I love you!" And she kissed the baby's head for the hundredth time. The baby smiled his first smile at her, and Magdalena saw a faint green aura about his head.

After farewells the next day, Magdalena and family boarded a riverboat bound upstream to Lugdunum, another Roman city. The rain having stopped, the sun shone hot on rows and rows of grape vines growing along the river. Late in the summer as it was, men and women worked in the vineyards, harvesting the black and yellow grapes.

"That must be where all that prime wine comes from," Zeno said. "I never tasted such wine as Bran poured for us at supper."

Eroica was thrilled to be on a river for the first time. Born at the seaside of Caesarea, she had never seen the river by which her mother had met her father. The Jordan, holy and life-giving as it was, didn't serve as a waterway like this river did. This river, the Rhodanus, was wide enough in some spots for two boats to pass each other. Eroica laughed at the water voles swimming along the banks and popping into their riverside burrows to hide from the boats. She never tired of seeing the villages and vistas that appeared around every turning. She felt the river's sacredness, especially when it ran through forests of ancient trees. Gaul seemed to her an enchanted place.

At Lugdunum, the party disembarked with their baggage and hired a cart to take them across land to the river Liger. The Romans intended to build a canal to link the two rivers. Such a link would speed trade across Gaul, bringing tin, hides, and grain from Britannia to the insatiable markets in Rome, but for now, the road was the only link between the two rivers. The trip by cart on the graveled road rattled their bones, but they reached the second river alive. The new boat was captained by a rough and shaggy fellow named Carmo. He swilled wine and made crude jokes with the passengers all day.

The only good thing about Carmo was his dog, who had a brood of puppies Eroica watched happily as the boat made its way westward, downstream. When one of the pups came loose from the mother's teat, Eroica would help it find its way back. She noticed that one pup was small and too weak to fight its way to the teat. When it did find a nipple, the mother turned her head and pushed it away.

Shocked, Eroica ran to the captain. "Sir, the mama dog keeps pushing the littlest pup away."

"That's the runt. She knows he won't make it, so she pushes him away. Here, I'll deal with him." Carmo then stepped to the box that held the bitch and her pups, picked up the runt and threw it overboard.

Eroica screamed. "No, you can't do that!" Then she jumped overboard herself and swam to the pup, who was weakly trying to keep his head above the stream.

The passengers shouted and looked at the girl dropping behind the boat as it continued downstream. Magdalena and Mary prayed.

"Damned brat," said Carmo. "Here, grab this." And he threw a wooden bucket to Eroica, holding the end of the rope that was tied to the bucket. Eroica had the pup in one hand, holding his nose above water, and couldn't swim well with only one arm, but she made it to the bucket, deposited the pup inside, and held on while Carmo pulled her in. "Stupid girl. That pup is going to die anyway. You can't save it."

"Yes, I can, and I will," Eroica said, setting her jaw. She had no idea how, but she set about to save Runt, as she called her pup. "Papa," she prayed, "help me save Runt. He is an outcast. You always save the outcasts. Help me. Amen."

Zeno heard the prayer as did Joseph. Joseph handed

her his stole to wrap the shivering puppy in. In the small hold of the boat, Zeno had seen a mother cat with a litter of kittens around her. Carmo kept a cat to kill the rats who entered his boat at the riverside docks. The cat was unlikely to suckle a pup, but the bitch would never take her own runt back now.

"Come, Eroica, let's see if the cat mama will help." Eroica approached the cat, softly cooing a kind greeting. She gently laid the pup near a vacant teat on the cat's belly. The cat only had four kittens, so there was space for Runt. Runt latched onto the cat's nipple, and she turned to look. She didn't seem to mind another kitten joining her litter, and Runt nursed there until the boat reached the mouth of the Liger at Portus Namnetum, on the northern sea.

"Thank you, God. Thank you, Papa," Eroica said. She had gained many things from traveling on the rivers of Gaul. The best one was Runt.

Chapter 15

Glastonbury

The party put up at an inn for the night, and Eroica begged some bread and milk from the cook to feed Runt. He didn't know to drink from the bowl, so she dipped her fingers in the sop and Runt sucked it off as best he could. He was happy to rest in Eroica's hands or in her lap. Magdalena watched her daughter's healing love pouring into the tiny dog and prayed for his survival. The next day, they boarded a ship bound for Britannia.

Mary didn't enjoy the crossing, for the sea tossed the ship dreadfully and made her ill. Eroica laid her hand on her grandmother to calm her. Rougher than the Mediterranean, the northern sea was gray and brooding, not blue and sunny. Little Runt cried and whimpered all the way, making everyone anxious. Finally, the ship came in sight of the harbor at Cala and docked.

"Only one more leg to go," Joseph said, trying to

encourage the tired travelers.

"Isn't this Britannia?" Zeno asked.

"Yes, but we have to go upriver to Glastonbury, our final destination. Come, let's find a boatman to take us," and Joseph spoke to a man on the dock in a language none of the others understood. "This fellow will take us. He thinks he can deliver us there before dark. The tide is coming in and will push us upstream a good ways, he says. Let's get on board."

The river flowed between limestone cliffs and even through a cave in the limestone at one point. The boatman, skilled and brave, kept his rowers in good heart by singing rhythmic songs and shouting encouragement. No one but Joseph knew the words of his song, but the melody soothed them, even Runt, who slept on Eroica's lap. Darkness was falling when they entered a large, reedy lake that had an island in the middle of it. In the center of the island stood a tall, conical hill.

"This is it. We are here. Glastonbury, our new home," Joseph said, paying the boatman.

Magdalena looked about her in the half light. After all the fine Roman cities they had traveled through, Glastonbury was a shock. Not a city at all, but a collection of round huts made of sticks met her gaze. Fires glowed through the doors and smoke arose through the roofs. Most of the inhabitants had retired for their suppers and bed.

"Follow me," said Joseph. "Let's see if the Oak can put us up." Zeno picked up Eroica to carry her, and Magdalena brought up the rear, after Mary. The Oak was a large roundhouse with other outbuildings. Joseph called out to the proprietor, "Hello, have you any room for weary travelers?"

A tall, white-skinned man came forward, took one look at Joseph and grinned. "Joseph! You're back. Where is Yeshua? Did you bring him with you?" He clapped Joseph on the arm then embraced him like an old friend.

"No, Jaffrez, Yeshua is not with me, but I brought his mother. Mary, this is Jaffrez, the host of this tavern. And I brought his wife, Magdalena." Jaffrez bowed to her. "And this is his daughter, Eroica, and her dog, Runt."

The tall innkeeper knelt down to see Eroica and Runt. "Oh, dear, that wee pup is in need of feeding. I'll take you to your beds and bring you all food." Jaffrez led them to one of the outbuildings and lit the fire in the center of the dirt floor. "I will be right back."

Mary's face looked gray. She still suffered after the sea crossing, so Magdalena urged her to lie down on the bed provided. Eroica sat near her, comforting the limp Runt. Soon, Jaffrez returned with his wife and baskets of food.

"This is my wife, Kwyn. She has made you a feast of lamb roast, bread, apples, and some mead. Now let me see this pup." Jaffrez sat down and showed Eroica how to feed the dog with a hollow reed. He dipped the reed into a cup of milk, put his finger over the end, then lifted the reed full of milk to Runt's lips. When he removed his finger from the reed end, the milk flowed into Runt's mouth. Runt took it willingly. Jaffrez handed the cup and reed to Eroica, who fed the pup till he fell contentedly asleep. Kwyn graciously handed around the dishes of food and poured cups of mead for all. When Magdalena tasted it, she jolted. It was sweet but very strong, much stronger than wine.

Kwyn noticed and smiled. She said something kind in her own language and left the hut. She returned with some apple cider, only mildly alcoholic, which the

ladies drank gladly. The men enjoyed the mead. All of
them would sleep well that night after the strong drink
and the long journey. They felt like they could breathe
now, since they had reached their new home.

Before he left them, Jaffrez said, "I will send my
boy over to Arveragus's first thing in the morning. He
will want to see all of you, I am sure. Good sleep."

"Who is Arveragus?" Zeno asked.

"He is the king. He has something to give me,"
Joseph said, and covered himself on his bed. The night
was dark and still. No city bustle filled the air, only the
gentle lapping of water in the reeds.

"Good morning, all," Kwyn called into the hut. "I've
brought you some breakfast and some news. Arveragus
wants to see you as soon as you are up and around. He
wants to hear your tidings and give you your gift, he
says."

Magdalena smiled, took the breakfast, and said,
"Thank you, Kwyn" before she realized that she had
understood the foreign tongue the woman spoke. What
was happening? "Mary, did you understand what Kwyn
said?"

"Yes, as if she spoke to me in my own language."

"I did, too, Mama. It's magic," Eroica said.

"I don't understand it."

"We don't need to. Just let it be, Mama. Maybe God
is helping us. Maybe Papa is. It's good. Now, where is the
reed? I need to feed Runt."

After eating and washing in the warm water
Kwyn brought, the party dressed as best they could and
followed Joseph across the town to the house of the king.
It was far from being a palace, just a bigger thatched
house with more outbuildings and barns around it. The
only outward sign of wealth was a large paddock full of

beautiful horses beside one of the barns. Eroica spoke to the horses as they approached, and they turned toward her and came to the side of the paddock. They snorted and tossed their shining heads in greeting.

"They say they love us, they love their life, and they love God. Just like the dolphins. Oh, how I like animals!" Runt squeaked in her pocket, and Eroica patted him. "Yes, especially my little Runt."

Arveragus had been on the lookout apparently, because he met them in front of his house as they neared.

"Joseph, my old friend!" he called. "Welcome home. Come in and let me meet your family. Come in. Come in."

Stepping inside the large roundhouse, Magdalena smiled to see that Arveragus had collected his entire clan to meet the newcomers. Arveragus introduced his wife, Queen Alys, his three tall sons Eppenos, Alan, and Brennus, as well as two daughters, Berit and Innogen. Arveragus gestured that they should sit on the leather slung wooden chairs around the room, and the daughters brought mead and cider.

"Thank you, Arveragus, for welcoming us so warmly. Allow me to introduce Mary, the mother of Yeshua. Magdalena, his wife. Zeno, her servant and a disciple of Yeshua. And Eroica, Yeshua's daughter."

Arveragus drew in his breath and walked over to Eroica, taking her small hand. "So this is the offspring of Yeshua. The gods be praised. She has that light in her eyes that he has. Why is he not with you?"

Then Joseph had the painful task of narrating the story of Yeshua's arrest and crucifixion. He carried on to tell his version of the resurrection and the appearances of the master after his rising, adding some of the more exalted phrases that had started circulating among the followers in Jerusalem. Magdalena was startled to hear Joseph say her husband was the only son of God, the Messiah, that he was ruling from heaven at the right hand of God, and other exaggerations she had never herself uttered. Of course, she hadn't been in the boiling mix of arguments among the followers for over five years while she raised Eroica in the relative peace of Caesarea. All sorts of different camps had devised their own shibboleths and jargon to tell the tale of her beloved. She knew him best, and these claims rang hollow to her. But she kept her peace, and let Joseph continue.

"So, you had to flee for your safety?" Arveragus said.

"Yes. We especially want to protect the child," Joseph said.

"The children are very sacred to us. We must celebrate Eroica and keep her living and thriving. Oh, but first, we must make her pup thrive. Brennus, take Eroica and her pup to the barn and see if someone will feed him. Perhaps one of the ewes."

"Yes, Father. Will you come with me, Miss?" Brennus said, and led her out to the sheep shed.

"The girl talks to animals, I believe?" Arveragus said.

"She hears them talk back, too. Birds, horses, dolphins, whales. It's uncanny."

"No, it is a gift. You have brought her to the right place. I predict she will shine in school and be a teacher herself before long," Arveragus said.

Magdalena wondered what school the king meant, but said nothing. Though the queen and her daughters sat in the room as part of the family, Magdalena wasn't sure yet how these tribes ranked their women. Did women speak up? Did anyone listen to the women here? She would wait and watch.

"Now, Joseph, I believe I owe you a hide of land. You earned it during your training here on your last visit. And Yeshua also earned his hide, but both of you had to leave before I could award it to you. I will show you the two hides today, and tomorrow we will celebrate with a feast your arrival to take your property in hand. The other hide we will award to Magdalena, honored wife of Yeshua and bearer of his child. I have set aside the land on which Yeshua built his small hut when you were here before. That land can be yours or Magdalena's, as you choose. The hut, I am afraid, is in ruins.

"On a day about five years after you left us, at the time of the complete solar eclipse, someone set fire to the thatch on your hut. I pulled down the burning thatch, but that left the rest of it open to the elements, and it's quite a mess now."

"There was a solar eclipse that day? Was there also a shaking of the earth?" Joseph asked.

"Yes, both happened on the day your hut burned."

Joseph looked at Mary and Magdalena, wide-eyed. "Arveragus, that was the day Yeshua was crucified. The sun went dark and the earth shook." The queen and her daughters covered their mouths to keep from crying out. Magdalena realized that all these people knew and loved her husband. They had lived with him from the time he was twelve or thirteen until he left them to return to Palestine at twenty-eight. They had been his family much longer than she had been. Her heart went out to them.

"Oh, my. We have much to celebrate and much to mourn. But you say Yeshua is risen? Let it be celebration, then. We, too, believe the soul is immortal and will come again, as you know, Joseph. We have this world for a time and the Otherworld for a time, and then we are reborn in this world. It is all life. Death is nothing. We shall celebrate tomorrow. Now, let's collect Eroica and the pup, and we will see your land."

In the shed, they found Runt vigorously nursing from a ewe who had only one lamb. Her teat was too big for a dog Runt's size, but the determined pup did his best.

"Eroica, you can leave him here to feed, or bring Runt along," Arveragus said. She started to leave him, but he came to her when he saw her turn to walk away. "Ah! Good choice, pup. Stay with the holy girl. You can feed more later." And the king led them to the paddock to mount their horses.

None of them had ridden any animal taller than a donkey, and Eroica hadn't done that. Magdalena suddenly missed her donkey Sophia, but she wasn't afraid, if one of the king's sons could help her up. Mary asked to be excused from riding. She returned to the house to be entertained by the queen and her daughters. Mostly, the women wanted to hear of the life of Yeshua from his mother's mouth. Prince Eppenos helped Magdalena mount her mare and put Eroica and Runt in front of her. Joseph and Zeno had some trouble, but managed to mount. The king and all his sons rode easily as accomplished horsemen do.

"Mama, horses are higher than I thought," Eroica said. "Hello, dear horse, I hope we are not too heavy for you. We promise not to whip you." The mare nodded her head as if in answer. For the rest of the day, the mare went gently and carefully, carrying the wife and child of Yeshua, and their dog.

Magdalena had no idea what a "hide" of land was. As they rode the boundaries of one property and then the other, she realized what a lavish gift the land was. Either one was large enough to hold a big house, barns, paddocks and pens, a kitchen garden, grazing land, and an orchard of apple trees or grape vines. Both hides had streams flowing across them, large oak and birch trees shading the edges of green grass fields, and one had the fallen hut Yeshua had built. She yearned to own that hide, even though part of it was low-lying and marshy.

"So, Niece, which hide do you choose? I bet I can guess," Joseph said, after they had seen both parcels.

"The one with the hut my beloved built," she said.

"Ha-ha! I knew it," Joseph laughed.

"Over it, I want to build a chapel. Inside we can teach what Yeshua taught and spread the good news."

Joseph took a deep breath. "My dear, I will help you build it. We will be making the first chapel that doesn't have to be hidden underground or behind closed doors. It will be out in the open for all to see and come to. What a wonderful idea!"

"I predict you will have many willing students. Better make it large," the king said. "Now, let us return to the house and share our news with the family. And you will stay with us as our guests until your own houses are built. The little pup will be happy in the sheep shed. Ha-ha!" And Arveragus set off, galloping towards home, with the new horsemen and horsewomen lagging behind.

Chapter 16

University

After two years of living in Britannia, Magdalena and her family had settled in. King Arveragus sent his workmen to help Joseph and Zeno build dwellings. Magdalena, Mary, Eroica, Zeno, and Runt lived on her land in a round, thatched house made of wattle and daub. Eroica watched the men set the poles into the ground and weave horizontal branches through them. When it came time to plaster the wattle with the muddy daub, Eroica helped. She loved putting her small hands into the wet goo and smearing it on the wood frame. Surprisingly, her childish efforts made good progress, and the men were glad of her help. Joseph built a smaller house by the same method on his land, along with a barn. Runt, who had thrived on the ewe's milk, also helped by fetching branches and bringing them to the site from the woods. Whatever Runt's breed, his puppyhood in the sheep shed had made him a good dog for herding and guarding the sheep. Joseph's farm had a goodly flock, and Runt had learned to respond to the shepherd's whistles and shouts. The two farms were adjacent, and Runt had the run of both, sharing the lives of all his favorite people.

One rainy day, when the family were gathered in Magdalena's house, Joseph broached his new project.

"Now that we have roofs over our heads, I would like to start work on the chapel. We will need to remove the fallen hut, and I would like to lay a stone floor."

"Can I help with the daub?" Eroica asked.

"Oh, yes, we need you on that task, young lady. May I have your blessing to begin, Magdalena?"

"Yes, how large are you planning it to be? Will it be round?"

"No, I want it to be rectangular, like a temple. I'd like to use larger posts at the corners and fill in with the wattle. Do you think that's possible?"

Zeno nodded. "Of course. With the axes and saws I am making in my forge, we can fell some hefty trees and make the chapel last centuries." Zeno had built a small hut near the marshy area of Magdalena's land and had set up a forge for metal working. The town flocked to his forge for all kinds of tools and implements as well as weapons. Daggers and swords were his specialty, but he also made some bronze bracelets and neck ornaments that the ladies liked. Zeno had gone to artisan school when he first arrived in Glastonbury. He had learned to compose songs and write poems, but he shone at metal working, so he concentrated on his strongest skill. He was proud to contribute to the household.

Druids established one of their universities in Glastonbury. People came from all over the known world to teach and to learn under the Druid masters. The artisan school taught rune-writing, poetry, music, dance, drawing, basketry, and working of wood and metal. The healing school taught herbal lore, potion mixing, casting spells, reading signs, prayer, bone-setting, surgery, midwifery, cooking, and brewing. The wisdom school taught justice, decision making, leadership, peace-making, astronomy, and foreign tongues. A master Druid usually took twenty years to learn the curriculum by heart. Yeshua had attended for sixteen years, in the healing and wisdom schools, mostly.

"Mama, now that I'm seven, can I start school? I want to learn what Papa learned when he was here."

Magdalena looked across at Joseph. She knew that women in Glastonbury were treated as equal to men, and many women attended the schools. She herself had been learning in the healing school for nearly a year now. However, she was unsure if a seven-year-old would be admitted.

"Well, Eroica, we can ask the master tomorrow. What do you want to study first?"

"Everything! I want to learn to write runes like Papa Zeno does. He already taught me a little. And I want to draw. Then, I want to learn to heal in the healing school. When I am older, I will learn about peace-making. I want to be the first woman Prince of Peace!" She beamed at her elders as she sat rubbing Runt's belly.

Some people called the king the Prince of War and the master Druid the Prince of Peace. He had been known to walk out into the middle of a battle, raise his arms, and stop the fighting by urging the parties to talk to each other. Part of what students learned in wisdom school was the futility of war, especially between local kings who fought over territory, cattle, or brides. The fine art of negotiation set the Prince of Peace apart from the warlike tribes surrounding him on all sides.

"Well, you be sure to tell that to the master when you see him tomorrow," Joseph said.

"Oh, I will!" Eroica said.

Just then a plaintive child's voice called through the doorway, which was hung with a cow hide to keep the cold out.

"Rowy! Is Rowy home? I need her spit."

Eroica went to the door.

"Come in, Alby. What's wrong?"

"I was jumping from a tree, and a splinter went into my leg." Eroica looked at the bloody bit of broken-off stick piercing her friend's leg. "I brought you some mud," and he held out his shaky hand full of black mud.

"Well done," she said, taking the mud into her own hand where she spat into it three times and mixed it with her finger. "Papa, please heal Alby's hurt. Amen." Then she smeared the mud on the wound, including the sliver. "Now, hold your hand over the mud till you are home, let it dry, then peel it off."

"Thanks, Rowy," and the tyke left the house.

The four adults looked at the girl and at each other.

"Is that the first time you've used mud to heal?" Mary asked her granddaughter.

"No, I always use mud when there's a thorn or a splinter. It pulls the thorn right out. If there's no thorn, I just use spit. It works on scrapes, stings, and black eyes." Eroica continued petting Runt, who was happy to lie under her care for as long as she kept petting him.

Zeno started to laugh. Then Mary laughed. Then Eroica laughed.

"What are we laughing at, Papa Zeno?"

"You, sweetheart. How long have you been

doctoring all the children in town?"

"Once I made friends, I started fixing them up. I hate to see anybody hurt, so I help them. It's easy."

"Does it always work?"

"No. They have to ask me. If I just go up and help them, it doesn't work. They have to believe I can help them. It always works then."

"Do many of them call you Rowy?"

"Yes, they all do. Eroica is such a long name, and some of them can't say it. I like the name Rowy. It sounds like friendship. Runt needs to go outside. Come on, boy," and out the door the little healer went.

The next day, Joseph took Eroica by the hand and walked with her to one of the large roundhouses of the university. Inside sat the master Druid in a circle with other teachers and learners. Among them sat a man with a white turban on his head, a long white beard, and brown skin. Near him was another man with black skin, dressed in bright colored robes. Eroica had never seen anyone like them, even in the market in Caesarea. When she and Joseph entered, all eyes turned to them. Joseph bowed to the master.

"Master, I am Joseph, uncle of Yeshua, formerly of this school."

"I remember you, Joseph. I heard of the death of Yeshua and his wonderful rising. Who is this young person? May we meet her?"

"Yes, this is Eroica, daughter of Yeshua. She is just seven years old, and she wants to know if she is too young to enter the school."

"Age is an illusion. If she wants to learn, she may enter the school. Eroica, what do you want to study?"

"Sir, I want to learn to write runes, draw, heal people, and bring peace to the world."

"Indeed. Well your father took only sixteen years to complete our curriculum. How long do you want to take?"

"Sir, may I just start and see how I go along? I am not wise enough yet to name a time."

The Druids, the brahmins, and the shamans smiled or chuckled their amusement.

"I think you speak wisdom already, young person. You are welcome to attend any classes you feel ready for. I suggest rune-writing and foraging for healing plants."

"Yes, sir. Thank you, sir. Can I begin today?"

One of the female Druids spoke up from the circle. "Yes, my rune class begins at noon, in the holy wood. Bring a short, sharp stick."

"Thank you. I will!" Eroica said, jumping for joy. Joseph bowed them out of the room, and they headed to the woods to seek a stick.

"Uncle Joseph, who was that man with a white beard? Where was he from?"

"He is from India, a land far across the world. Your father loved to talk with the learned men from India. And did you notice the black skinned man? He is from Africa, a land to the south."

"Do all those people pray to God?"

"They use different words and they picture different images in their minds, but in the end they all pray to the same God, our God, because there is only one. People who pray to many gods are really praying to aspects of the one God. I don't think God minds. God knows we have trouble with God's bigness and invisibility."

"Will I be learning those things in school?"

"Yes, you will be learning those things and much more. And don't forget that you have your own ideas to add to the school. In this school, every student has a voice. Sharing his ideas with the others is what made your father such a good preacher."

"Will I be a preacher some day, Uncle Joseph?"

"If you wish to be and learn your lessons, I think you will make a good preacher. Or teacher, or poet, or artist, or mother, or doctor, or farmer, or dog-trainer. There are many paths to choose, my dear."

"But how will I choose? I think I will like them all."

"Your heart will tell you, and you can always talk to your father in heaven."

"Oh, yes, Uncle. I talk to him every day, and he always gives me good advice. Here's a good stick," she said, picking a stick from the forest litter underfoot.

"Well chosen. Let's take it to Papa Zeno to sharpen. Then you have your first class."

Later, when she returned home from rune class, Eroica swept aside the floor rushes and drew her lesson in the dirt of the floor.

"See, Grandmary, all the runes are shaped like a tree. They have different branches, twigs, and fruits. That's what makes them mean different things."

"I think you did well for your first lesson. Your friend Alby came by to show us his wound. The splinter was gone and the skin healed."

"Oh, good. Thank you, Papa," she said, looking to heaven. "Mama, tomorrow I am going foraging. Do you want to come?"

"Indeed. There are still some plants I don't know about. I'll be glad to hear what your teacher has to say about them. Once you master herbal cures, you will be an extraordinary healer, my daughter. I am very proud of you."

"Thank you, Mama. Papa says he is proud, too."

Magdalena smiled a bittersweet smile and embraced her girl.

Chapter 17

Chapel

In the rectangular thatched chapel, listeners sat in rows and the speaker stood up to teach. Joseph presided over the lessons when Druid learners came to the chapel to hear about Yahweh and Yeshua. One day a week, on either Saturday or Sunday, the whole family taught. Mother Mary told her story, Zeno repeated the parables he had learned at Yeshua's feet, and Magdalena spoke of the teachings her husband had shared with her. Even Eroica stood up to convey the latest message she had heard from her Papa in heaven. Those psalms they knew by heart were sung, prayers of thanks and intercession were said, and Zeno provided a simple meal.

Over the meal, sometimes people asked questions and discussed their different views of the divine. One of the female Druids pointed out that their view of the godhead was a trinity: The creator father, the nature mother, and the daughter earth.

"Is your God unified as one?" she asked.

"Yes," Magdalena said. "Our God is a spirit. Many of us use the word 'he' to refer to God, but God is not a man."

Zeno asked, "Why do Druids not write down all the wisdom you teach in the university? Are you not worried it will be lost?"

"Writing it down is no guarantee it will not be lost. We lock it into our memories for safe keeping. We write down histories and records, but we keep the secret knowledge in our memories. We value the strength of memory and feel it will be weakened by writing things down."

Magdalena thought how sacred memory became. She had not brought any written scriptures when they left so suddenly from Caesarea. The beginnings of Yeshua's story that Eunice had started recording had been left in Magdala. She resolved to make a start writing down all she had been teaching in the chapel as well as other stories of her brief life with Yeshua. Though the followers of Yeshua in Glastonbury had a visible chapel and were allowed to share their understanding of God, there were no guarantees that they would not be attacked at some later date. In her tradition, people wrote down the words of God and about God.

She looked around the chapel and noticed that those who attended were mostly the elite of the Druid university. Druids, poets, and healers of both sexes were there, but no farmers, traders, or peasants came. Female common folk were conspicuously absent. How blind she had been. In her heart she heard her husband's voice saying "that we all may be unified." On the walk back to their farm, Magdalena spoke.

"Joseph, we are not spreading the good news

to the common folk. Yeshua loved the poor and the forgotten. Why are we not feeding them God's love? And the women. Mother, don't you think we could have a New Moon School again, for all the women, not just the Druid students?"

"Yes, I think the women would be happy to come," Mary said.

"And I can help," Eroica bubbled. "When is the next new moon? Grandmary, we can bake some cakes!"

Joseph scowled. "I suppose you can have a common women's school, but please don't hold it in the chapel."

"Why not, Uncle? Are women not allowed?" Eroica asked.

Joseph looked ashamed. "No, I didn't mean that. But we can't spare the chapel for three days in a row. Maybe one day in the chapel?"

Magdalena smiled. "We will arrange it to suit everyone. We just need to love our neighbors better than we have been. That message came through clearly to me."

Joseph kept busy at the university, Zeno worked in his forge, and the women were left to start the New Moon School. Carrying baskets of fresh-baked honey cakes, Magdalena and Eroica set off to invite all the women in town for the first meeting at the new moon. They started at the Oak Inn since they knew Kwyn. She answered their call with a pan in her hand. She was whisking eggs with a bunch of twigs tied together.

"Magdalena, what a surprise," Kwyn said. "Come into the kitchen. I'm making a custard."

"Yummy, that will go well with the cakes we brought you," Eroica said, holding out the basket.

"Well, thank you, child."

"We want to invite you to the first meeting of the New Moon School, at our farm a week from tomorrow."

"Oh, my dear, on the first night of the new moon, we have a ritual in the holy wood."

"What is the ritual?" Magdalena asked.

"The women meet and have a fire to encourage the moon to come back. We drink mead or cider, dance a little, let our hair down, and celebrate that we are alive for another month. You should come. You'd be very welcome. Bring Mary, too."

"Do you think the women would come to my farm after?" Magdalena asked.

"Some of them are too much in their cups and end up sleeping in the wood all night, but you can ask them. If you offer cakes like these, you will have some takers, I'm sure," Kwyn said, smiling.

"Do all the women come to the ritual? Rich and poor?" Magdalena asked.

"More poor than rich, I'd say. The king's ladies sneak out in masks sometimes to join us, but it's not considered proper for high-born women. The women students join us, though. It's a mixed group."

"Wonderful! That's what we want, right, Eroica?"

"Yes, we want all the ladies. Girls, too."

"I will spread the word to any women who come by the tavern that the ritual will have two parts---one in the wood and one at your place afterwards."

"Thank you, Kwyn!"

"I thank you for the cakes. Good-bye."

Eroica and her mother stopped in at a few more houses until the cakes were gone. They hoped that the grapevine of gossip would spread the invitation to the rest of the town's women, and sure enough, their hopes bore fruit.

Excitement ran high on the night of the ritual. Kwyn assured Magdalena that the group was larger than usual, and Magdalena could see for herself that a good cross-section of the community were there: farm wives, shop keepers, students, peasant women, and the king's daughters, hanging back in the shadows of the trees. Torches and the bonfire lighted the scene. Eroica joined a ring of girls chanting and spinning in a laughing dance. Women chatted and embraced, sharing apple cider and wine made from currants. Some of the women sprinkled wine on the trees as another said a prayer of thanksgiving to the earth. Mary and Magdalena felt welcome and at home among them. Magdalena could feel God's love flowing from person to person and all around the holy wood.

As Kwyn had predicted, some women fell asleep in the leaves and couldn't be roused to walk to Magdalena's. Some had to return to their husbands and farms. But about half of the revelers walked in a jovial procession, carrying their torches, to Magdalena's, where they ate their fill of Zeno's good cooking. After, they bedded down around the central fire and slept a worry-less sleep, safe and well fed, with no chores to do since breakfast would greet them in the morning, ready-made.

"Thank you for this, Magdalena," Kwyn said. "It's not often women enjoy this kind of pampering. You bless us all." Magdalena smiled, thinking of the even greater blessing she would give them in the morning.

After breakfast, Magdalena asked the women to sit in a circle in her round house. Used to circles for worship and learning, the women were perfectly comfortable doing so. They looked to Magdalena, whom they knew to be a healer and the wife of a prophet, to hear what she could tell them.

"I want to tell you the good news that my husband Yeshua taught when he was alive," she began. "One time he gave a talk, standing on a hill, in which he said that the poor, the lowly, the outcasts, and the meek people were blessed. He promised that God loves all people equally, whether they are men or women, children or elders, rich or poor, strong or weak. If people are suffering in this life, they are bound to be rewarded in the Otherworld."

One of the students spoke up. "Do you say that souls come back from the Otherworld to live here again?"

"Some of us say that. We look forward to a day of resurrection when all the people who have lived will come alive."

"All at once?"

"Some say so."

"We say they come back one at a time, being placed in a new body."

"But we agree that the soul never dies," Magdalena said.

The women nodded.

"Yeshua also said the peace-makers are blessed, and I know that your masters are called Prince of Peace. We have that in common."

"Yes, we know peace is right, but our men still insist on making war. They employ the Druids to help them in battle, reading signs for battle omens and casting spells for good weather."

"Yeshua would say to forgive them. God forgives us for all the selfish things we do, and God wants us to do that for our neighbors, too. Forgiveness is a big part of Yeshua's teaching. We are not to seek revenge; it's part of peace-making."

"So, will forgiving guarantee that we are rewarded in the Otherworld?"

"No. God wants to reward you anyway. What it will do is make life here in this world better, letting go of bitterness. If you forgive your enemies and give thanks for what you have, your heart can be at peace now. I see your people living this way already. You are always giving thanks to the gods for nature and all of the creation around you. You are blessed with plenty of water, growth, trees, animals, and beauty. Do you see how much the gods love you?"

"Yes. But you have only one god. Does your god love us, too, even though we don't sacrifice to him...her... it?"

"Yes. We see God as one, and we see God as love. If love is there, God is there. I see love among your people, and therefore you are blessed. What name we give God is less important than being grateful. We call it the sacrifice of thanksgiving---that's the only sacrifice our God asks for."

"Really? No animals or coins thrown into the bog? Do you do any rituals at all?"

"We break bread together, and when we drink the wine, we remember Yeshua. Yeshua told us just before he left us not to burden ourselves with a lot of rules and rituals."

"Wine ritual! That sounds good," Kwyn said, lightening the mood. "Jaffrez just got a shipment of Greek wine last week. I should have brought some!"

The women laughed, and Magdalena let that be the end of her talk. She had said enough.

"My sisters, I look forward to celebrating with you at the next new moon. Thank you all for coming.

You have blessed me with your presence." The women embraced Magdalena and each other before taking their leave. Some kissed her cheek. Others held her hand and smiled into her eyes. Indeed, love prevailed in the town of Glastonbury, and God blessed them all.

Interest in the good news as taught by Yeshua exploded after the first New Moon School. More and more women came to the ritual and Magdalena's house each month. More poor men and women began to attend meetings in the chapel, drawn by the message of God's love for them. A few of the head Druids seemed put off by the presence of the lowly folk and started missing meetings, which saddened Magdalena. Not only did Yeshua preach the unification of the heart within the person, but the unification of all types of people under the umbrella of God's love. Some people didn't want to share the umbrella. Joseph, Mary, Magdalena, and Zeno shared the chapel teaching between them. Zeno, maybe because the poorer people saw him as one of the common folk, had a huge following and became well known in Glastonbury and the nearby villages. It came to pass that within two years of the crucifixion of Yeshua, a thriving colony of his followers were living the realm of God, in their little corner of Britannia.

Chapter 18

Tor

Though Magdalena loved talking about Yeshua and his ideas in the chapel and at the new moon, she didn't teach visioning in Glastonbury the way she had in Magdala. The Druids had their own methods of divination by reading signs, and they practiced silent prayer of a sort under the oak trees. In fact, Joseph told her that Yeshua had learned the practice in university from the Druids. Therefore, she dropped the imagination lessons from her curriculum, telling herself her students didn't need them. One morning, she awoke after a dreamless sleep to realize that the reason she didn't want to teach visioning was that her own visions had stopped. Since she left Caesarea, she had had some ordinary dreams, but nothing prophetic, and no daytime visions. She shared her pain over this loss with her friend Nevanthi, who taught healing and herbal lore at the university.

"You need to climb the Tor," Nevanthi said. "Closer to heaven, closer to vision. That's what I always say."

So Magdalena walked alone up the spiral terrace that encircled the green Tor, climbing slowly to the top. The grassy path was wide enough for a procession of worshipers walking three abreast. She had seen these processions at the four main feasts of the year, but she had yet to participate in one. As she climbed, she looked out across the countryside, over the marshy lake that surrounded the island, over the fields of grain, and in the far distance, the misty sea.

Suddenly, her perceptions changed. Though she still looked abroad with natural eyes, the supernatural vision she used to know clicked into place. She had passed through a veil separating the earthly from the spiritual. Magdalena breathed a thank-you to God and kept walking uphill along the gentle curve.

Flashes of vision, only fragments, entered her ken. They didn't stay long enough for her to interpret, but they reassured her that Nevanthi had given her good advice. The Tor was a portal to the spirit. She saw Eroica dressed as a Druid priestess. She saw Mother Mary praying by a pool of dark water. She saw flames rising high into the sky.

Then she saw a tall, hooded figure descending the path toward her. Gowned in white, it appeared to be a Druid with his head down in deep meditation. He raised his head and looked at her. Her heart stopped. Yeshua's eyes locked onto hers, piercing to her soul. In that moment she felt his love, his yearning, and his eternal marriage to her. He was still with her. She had only to open the eyes of her heart.

Magdalena began to run, hoping to catch him in her arms, but when she was near enough to embrace him, the vision shifted and he was not Yeshua. He was Ahearn, one of the masters she knew from the university.

"Good day, Magdalena," he said, smiling. "Enjoy your walk." And he passed her by without further remark.

Stunned, she stood still, feeling the tears welling hot in her eyes. No, Yeshua was not really here. As her tears fell, a voice spoke in her left ear as if someone whispered behind her.

"Press on," it said.

She wiped her eyes and forced her legs to keep climbing in obedience to the voice. Early ancestors of the Britons had flattened the top of the Tor for large gatherings and celebrations, where bonfires burned. Sometimes signal fires burned on the top to warn of invading armies. She saw the blackened evidence of those fires. Circling the top of the hill, she felt a particularly strong pull at one spot opposite the burned place. She lay down on her back and closed her eyes. That's when the full vision came.

She sat with Mary and Eroica in her house when a man's voice called at the door. Mary went to draw aside the cowhide, admitting a huge, fierce man that Magdalena recognized as Judas. He pulled out his short sword and ran at Eroica who screamed and fled. Magdalena followed her from the house and the two of them ran up the path on the Tor, Judas following and yelling after them. Magdalena's feet could gain no purchase on the grassy slope, and she dropped behind her daughter, who kept climbing. Judas passed her, saying, "It's the girl I want" and continued up the hill. Then Magdalena was on top of the Tor, and she watched as Eroica jumped from the hilltop and flew over the lake, dropping into the dark water and disappearing. When she looked back, Judas was hanging from a tree, arms and legs splayed out in the shape of an X. Her mind couldn't take in what she saw, and she blinked to clear her vision. A noise of loud commotion called her attention to the ramp ascending the Tor, and she saw an army of Roman soldiers marching upward, carrying shields and banners. Their line stretched to the horizon. When she opened her eyes, she had one thought: flee.

She took a deep breath, and her heart called out to God. The reply came, "Fear not, I am with you." Yes, God was always with her, but her fear made her doubt. Always before, the visions had reassured, and if they warned, she knew without doubt whether they were true or not. This time, she questioned the vision. Was it a prediction of future events? Was it just a reflection of her general fears for Eroica's safety? She didn't know. "Fear not," God said. So she dismissed the vision and descended the Tor. All would be well.

———— • ————

When Eroica heard that her mother had climbed the Tor, she begged to do the same.

"Mama, take me with you up the Tor."

Magdalena hesitated to take her daughter up the hill because the energies were so strong. She knew Eroica felt cosmic and telepathic vibrations easily, and she feared to overwhelm the girl at the tender age of seven. But she relented, knowing Eroica's hardiness matched her sensitivity.

Reaching the hilltop, Eroica went straight to the spot where Magdalena had lain during her fearful vision.

"Mama, look, the grass is a different green over here. What do you suppose is underneath?" Eroica dug around the contrasting patch with her walking stick, revealing the edges of a rectangular wooden slab. "I wonder if I could pry it up. Maybe it's a door to secret treasure. I bet some old king buried gold here."

Magdalena laughed. The girl kept digging until she managed to insert the stick under the edge and dislodged the wood.

"It *is* a door, Mama. Come help me."

When the two had lifted the trap door, hinges creaking and clods of dirt dropping away, the top few steps of a staircase appeared. Musty air arose from the opening, and the layer of dust on the steps hinted that no one had passed that way for a very long time. Down into darkness the steps disappeared.

"Come on, Mama. Let's explore down there."

"Eroica, it will be dark when you go down a few steps. We don't have a torch or candle. We will have to come back another day."

"No, we won't. Come on. I'll show you," and the girl took her mother's hand and tugged her to the opening.

A few steps down, Eroica held her hand up, fingers separated, and tiny glints of light began to emanate from her fingertips. They gave enough light to enable Magdalena to see the steps further down.

"Daughter, what are you doing?"

"I am shining light. Papa says it's all right for me to do it in an emergency. This is an emergency, I think."

Thrilled at the sight of divine sparks flowing out of Eroica's hand, Magdalena made no objection and followed her down the steps. The steps turned, descended, and spiraled into the darkness. At one level, a cave opened up to the side, and they found the skeleton of a nobleman, perhaps a king. All of the burial treasures had been ransacked, leaving only the bones, a wooden burial wagon, and some scraps of cloth over the bones.

"See, I told you some old king buried gold here.

Somebody just stole it. Oh, well. Let's keep going!"

Several more flights and the staircase ended at another cave where they heard the sound of water trickling. Eroica stretched her hand out, and the light reflected off the surface of a hidden pool, deep and cold.

"Well, that's the end," Magdalena said. "Now we have to climb all those steps back up."

"No, Mama, I could swim out. I bet the pond has a stream flowing to the lake. Maybe it's one of the springs that come out of the Tor, the red one or the white one."

Still full of the fears lingering after her hilltop vision, Magdalena refused.

"Absolutely not! You have no idea where that goes. We are going back the way we came. Now."

"All right, Mama. Don't be angry," and Eroica obeyed, harboring hopes of another day, and another adventure.

The climb up the steps to the top of the Tor left them both breathless. Mother and daughter craved the dinner that awaited them at home. Neither told anyone about the secret stair or Eroica's lightmaking skills.

———————— • ————————

A few days later, Mary took a walk to the red spring, her favorite place to pray. Though Magdalena, Zeno, and Eroica liked praying Druid-style under oak trees, she preferred to be by water, and the locals held that the red and white springs were the abode of powerful spirits. Issuing from the base of the Tor, both springs were holy. The red one had a rusty tinge to the water and tasted like iron. The white one's water was clear, fresh tasting, and invigorating. Mary knelt among the ferns by the red spring and prayed aloud to God until tears came flowing from her eyes. As if in answer to her prayer, a water sprite bubbled up from the dark water and saluted her.

"Grandmary! It's me!" Eroica's wet head with hair swept back and bright smiling eyes confronted her, and she took in her breath.

"Oh! Child! You frightened me. Where did you come from?" Mary reached a hand to help the girl from the spring.

"There's a secret pool under the Tor. Don't tell anybody. Grandmary, why are you crying? Don't worry; I am safe."

"I know, sweeting. You are always safe in the water. I was crying for my other children and grandchildren. I will never see them again." She wiped her eyes. "Never mind. I'm being silly."

"No, Grandmary, love is never silly. Love is God. Let's go home. Mama can help you write a letter home to your family. And I can write one in runes! Uncle Joseph can send it by ship. When the answer comes back, you will know they are all well and happy." The girl helped her grandmother up, and they walked home.

Magdalena didn't scold Eroica for sneaking up the Tor. She had expected it would happen sooner or later. She was more concerned about Mary's sadness.

"Mother, of course we can write home to Galilee. I have some fine vellum the queen gave me after I helped cure her fever. That will make the journey safely. Let me get it."

"If you can have it done by tomorrow, I will take it to Jaffrez at the inn. A boat will be going down to Cala. If the letter sets sail with a ship this week, you might hear back in a month or two," Joseph said.

So the letter was written in Aramaic on vellum, directed in Greek to her son Jude, in Cana of Galilee. Eroica wrote runes in the margins. The runes formed a prayer for fair winds and safe travel. Never mind that her uncles and aunts in Galilee would not be able to read them; they made a lovely decorative border for Magdalena's fine hand. Eroica insisted on accompanying Joseph to the inn to put the letter into Jaffrez's keeping.

"Can we wait until the boat comes? I want to make sure Grandmary's letter is sent properly," Eroica said.

"No, dear girl. We need to go home for supper. We can come back tomorrow. There's no telling when the boat will arrive. You could be waiting all day."

"That wouldn't bother me, Uncle Joseph. I could help Kwyn make custard! I am a skilled egg-cracker." Joseph smiled and took her hand.

Supper was delayed by an unexpected arrival. Runt walked through the door carrying a tiny puppy in his mouth. Runt had fathered several litters of puppies on the bitches at Joseph's farm, and the clever dogs were much in demand by local shepherds. Joseph had even exported some of them to Gaul at a hefty price. Who could have predicted that the old tin-trader would become a dog-breeder?

"Come here, Runt," said Eroica. "What have you got?" Runt came to her and laid the tiny pup at her feet. The weak little mite could barely lift its head. "Is this the runt of your litter, boy? Do you want me to help him?" In his deep brown eyes the answer shone clear. Eroica picked up the tiny dog and cradled it. "I will do my best. Let's get him---oh, her---some milk," and she took the pup out to the sheep shed. If sheep's milk had turned Runt into the strong, handsome specimen he was, it was good enough for his little daughter.

Nursing the new runt kept Eroica busy, so she forgot about the letter to Galilee. Joseph assured Mary that Jaffrez had sent it. It only remained to await an answer.

Chapter 19

Samhain

By the time Eroica was ten, she had raised a dozen of Runt's runts. He brought her the tiniest, weakest pup of every litter, and she saved them all. When they were strong enough, she returned them to Joseph to be trained. She always had the latest pup under foot, and both Mary and Magdalena enjoyed having such playful companions about. Magdalena didn't encourage her daughter to make a pet of any of them. Sentimentality and clinging were traps she had learned to eschew.

Mary had enjoyed a steady, though slow, correspondence with her family back home. The vellum letters with runic embellishments traveled east, and papyrus replies came west after a few months. Sometimes Magdalena wrapped her missives in an extra sheet of vellum for Jude to use for his reply. Papyrus wasn't always easy to come by. News of new babies, some deaths, money worries, weddings, and political happenings came to the family in Britannia. Disputes and controversies among Yeshua's followers continued. A new fellow from Tarsus called Paul was making quite a stir. Apparently a vision of Yeshua had converted him, and he was traveling in Turkey spreading his version of the message. Magdalena wasn't worried. God would sort it out.

As October neared its end, Glastonbury buzzed with the Samhain preparations. Men carried wood to the top of the Tor for the great bonfire. Women cooked and baked, preparing the harvest feast. Barrels of beer and mead were rolled or carried up the Tor in preparation for the year's first festival, celebrating the end of the growing season and honoring the dead. Eroica asked Magdalena to braid her hair in a special way she had seen her friend Cait wearing.

"Cait says we have to sweep the house with a birch broom and set a place at the table for our dead ancestors. And bury some apples for them."

"Which of our ancestors would you set a place for?" Magdalena asked.

"Papa in heaven of course. I know he is always with me, but he will have an easier time talking to me on Samhain, Cait says. The line between earth and heaven thins out."

"So I have heard. Let's hope Cait is right. We don't have a birch broom. Do you want to collect some twigs from the wood?"

"Yes, Mama. I will go now, and I'll take the pup."

"I hope the weather holds," Zeno said, looking at the sky.

"Don't worry, Papa Zeno. I will pray for the rain to come after the festival," Eroica said.

"The Druids have cast some spells already," Joseph

said. "I heard them talking about it. They like to brag that it hasn't rained on the Samhain fire in fifty years. We shall see. And Magdalena, do you think you should indulge the girl by letting her follow all these pagan superstitions?"

Magdalena looked at Joseph, and for the first time she saw him as an old man. Haggard and slightly stooped, he spoke in the voice of old prejudices, old rules.

"I just remember Yeshua telling me not to draw lines to shut anyone out. Eroica will make up her own mind about the truth if we let her be herself. I'm trusting God and her Papa in heaven to keep her safe."

Joseph subsided. "Of course you are right. I think I will return to my house to rest up for the festivities." And Joseph swept aside the cowhide door and left, head down. Magdalena said a silent prayer for him within her heart.

The neighbors thought of the day beginning at sunset, so in the afternoon everyone set out for the Tor, carrying their food baskets, blankets, and babies on their hips. Before they left their homes, they extinguished their fires. They would bring down new fire from the Tor to re-light the home fire for the new year. Eroica insisted Magdalena follow the local custom.

"Zeno, will you go over to Joseph's and help him up the hill? He seemed poorly when he was here earlier, and he might need a hand," Magdalena said. "We will meet you on the Tor."

But when Zeno found Magdalena in the crowd at the hilltop, he was alone.

"Joseph asked us to excuse him. He isn't feeling well. I put some food and water by his bed and left him. I hope that was the right thing to do."

Mary overheard and looked worried. "He didn't seem himself. I will go to him."

"But Mother, you will miss the festival."

"I have attended enough parties in my lifetime. Family is more important. I will make him a tea with some of your willow bark. You young people enjoy yourselves." And Mary walked against the flow of revelers making their way up the hill, laughing and singing since they had already been at the beer.

Flames from the bonfire rose high over the Tor, carrying prayers to the heavens, asking the gods for protection during the upcoming winter. Some brave souls, especially boys, leaped across the flames expecting blessing from it. Eroica danced and chased around with her friends, playing catch with apples and throwing the cores into the fire.

Magdalena looked up, wondering if it were true that the barrier to heaven was thin tonight. Would Yeshua come to her? Suddenly, she wanted to go home.

"Zeno, I am taking some fire home to our hearth. Will you stay with Eroica and make sure she comes home safe?"

"Of course, my lady."

Magdalena lit a torch and walked down the ramp from the Tor. Stopping briefly in her own home, she lit the fire and banked it up. Then she took the torch on her way to Joseph's. As she made out the shape of Joseph's small house, she stopped in her tracks. Through the thatch of the roof, she saw two ghostly figures arise. Both shimmered and shifted, their edges blurry and greenish. She blinked her eyes hoping for clarity. The brighter one was leading the other, escorting it into the sky.

"Uncle Joseph!" she called. The face of the

second figure turned toward her as if he had heard. She recognized Joseph's smile. The figure raised a hand in gesture of farewell, and both apparitions flew up and disappeared. Magdalena ran as fast as she could in the dark and found Mary crying softly by the body of her uncle.

"He just went," Mary said.

"Yes, I saw an angel taking his soul away."

"Praise God. He was burning up with fever, and he had red spots on his chest. He couldn't catch his breath. Oh, my dear Joseph." Magdalena put her arm around Mary to comfort her.

"Come, Mother. Come home with me."

"No, I will stay and keep vigil. Zeno and some of the men can bury him tomorrow. He wants to be buried in the chapel. His last wish."

"But, Mother, you are exhausted. The angels will keep him safe. You need sleep."

"Daughter, don't argue. Leave me. I want to be here." So Magdalena returned home alone. She fell asleep, disturbed in the wee hours by the return of Eroica and Zeno, and awoke at dawn with the remnants of a dream in her head. She had seen a procession carrying two corpses toward the thatched chapel. Her heart began beating hectically, and she called out for Zeno.

"We have to go over to Joseph's. I've had a premonition." They both ran to Joseph's house in the chill of the morning. There on the floor next to Joseph's body lay Mary. His hand was clutched in hers. Red spots marked her neck, but her face was at peace.

Magdalena let out a wail from the depths of her body. She had never made such a sound, but she let it come. Joseph's farm hands came running from their hut to see what was wrong. Zeno led her outside. The men showed no surprise at the sight they beheld when they looked inside.

"It often happens like this on Samhain," one of them said. "It's an easy crossing to the Otherworld. A blessing, really. After a short time there, they will return. Never fear. Death is nothing."

Magdalena looked at him, speechless. How could he say death was nothing? She had just lost half of her family, all at once. Death was a thief, horrible. She laid her head on Zeno's chest and cried.

"Mama, what's wrong?" Eroica had walked over, sleepy-eyed, with the pup in the crook of her arm. Her hair was tousled, the braids having come out. Without waiting for an answer, she put her head past the door flap, saw the scene, and went to her mother.

"Never mind, Mama. I will take care of you. Let's go home." She led Magdalena by the hand. "Papa told me it will be all right. But I need to take care of you myself, nobody else."

Her mother looked at the girl quizzically. She always believed Eroica's pronouncements, but she didn't always understand them.

When the Druids of the university learned of Joseph's death, they began planning the funeral rites. The poets composed a processional song and elegies praising Joseph, Mary, and Yeshua. Drummers were hired to lead the procession, and gravediggers made two graves at the west end of the chapel floor. West, the direction of the setting sun and the entrance to the Otherworld, was the best spot.

"But Zeno, they should be buried before sunset."

"Who told you that? The Torah? It's not hot here; we can wait a day or two. If we let our Druid friends remember Joseph their way, we honor them. They want to bury goods in the graves, and they asked me what we wanted to bury."

"Ancient superstition," Magdalena scoffed. Then she remembered how she had accused Joseph of judging harshly the old traditions. "I'm sorry. Let them do as they please."

"I was thinking some tin dishes, since Joseph was a tin trader, and maybe Mary's letters from home. They want to bury a dog with Joseph."

"No!" Eroica said, big-eared as she came in the door. "I won't let them kill any dog for that."

"They think it will keep Uncle company in the Otherworld."

"Nonsense. We could put a dog-whistle in his grave. No real dogs."

But the perfect dog to send to the Otherworld volunteered. Runt, distraught at seeing the body of Joseph, lay down by his side and wouldn't leave. The next day, he was dead. Eroica cried tears for Runt, but made no objection to his joining Uncle in the grave. Somehow, the idea comforted her.

On the day of the double funeral, Zeno and Joseph's men carried the bodies on biers to the chapel. A procession of folks from the university and the town followed behind, keening and clapping their hands to the slow beat provided by the drummers. They couldn't all fit into the chapel, so the poet recited his poems in praise of Joseph and Mary outside the chapel door where the mourners gathered around. Mary's body went into the ground with her letters, her warmest shawls, flowers Eroica had picked for her, a jug of cider, loaves of bread and a bowl of apples. At the last minute, Zeno had fashioned two crosses of the silver he had been saving to make a gift for Magdalena. He laid one on Mary's chest, above her heart.

Joseph was laid with Runt, representing all the dogs he had bred during his time in Britannia. Tin dishes, candlesticks, a bronze dagger, a jug of mead, loaves of bread, a sheepskin, some coins, fragrant herbs Eroica had gathered, and a short poem written in runes on vellum were laid to rest with him. Finally, Zeno placed a cross on his chest.

Zeno, Magdalena, and Eroica said the psalm that starts "The lord is my shepherd" over the graves, and the mourners paid close attention. Everyone understood about shepherds, how they gave their lives for the sake of the weak and scattered. It was a good poem, worthy of a Druid poet. When the mourners left, the gravediggers filled the graves and replaced the stone floor over them. No engraving marked the stones. No one knew that the mother and uncle of Yeshua were buried in Glastonbury, and no one ever would.

Chapter 20

Assassins

By the time Magdalena reached her home, she was feverish. She dropped down on her bed and prayed.

"Mama, are you sick already? No one else must be near you, Papa said. Papa Zeno, you must live outside or at your forge. Nobody must touch Mama. You can bring us food, water, and wood, but leave it outside the door."

The child's commanding demeanor brooked no denial, and Zeno set off to gather what Eroica ordered. She bathed her mother's forehead with cool water and made her drink water she had boiled in an iron pot. She offered foods if Magdalena could stomach them, and she sang and chanted prayers to keep her mother's spirits up. In the night, Magdalena began to thrash and ramble in delirium, but Eroica kept praying and listening for her Papa's advice. All she heard was comfort and reassurance, so she knew she was doing the right thing. He told her that God had built the healing into Mama's body. All she needed was to allow the healing to happen. At the same time the thrashing ended, the red spots appeared. Was this a good sign or a bad one? Eroica shouted for Zeno.

"Papa Zeno! Will you run to Nevanthi and ask her if I should give Mama some herbs now? And what herbs? I think the fever has broken. She has stopped thrashing on the bed."

Zeno returned with Nevanthi herself, carrying an armful of fresh plants and a basket of dried herbs and mixed potions.

"Don't come in, please, Nevanthi. No one is to touch her but me. What did you bring? You can hand it to me through the door."

"I will have Zeno brew a tea of basil, willow bark and elderflower for the fever. And I will leave you a salve of calendula and nettle if her spots begin itching. If not, just leave them alone. Tomorrow, I will bring you some calves foot broth to build up her strength. You are doing a fine job, young lady. Here are some barley cakes for you. You must keep your strength up, too. I will return tomorrow to check on you both." And Nevanthi left, handing Zeno the tea makings.

After Magdalena drank the tea, she fell into a fitful sleep, and Eroica wrapped herself in a blanket by the fire and slept, too. Still disturbed by her weakness and fever, Magdalena had dreams that jumped and splintered. The scenes she saw made no sense, none of the places or figures familiar. At one point, she made the mental effort to erase her chaotic vision and clear away the confusion. When all was black, Yeshua came to her from deep in the darkness. He smiled as he strode toward her, but the closer he came, the more troubled grew his expression. Finally, he took her by the shoulders, shook her and said, "Go west. Do not fight them. Run." Then he kissed her lips and disappeared. Magdalena slept on, and in the morning she didn't remember the dream. All she remembered was the joy of seeing her daughter smiling down on her, proffering a cup of broth.

"Mama, you are better. Nevanthi brought you this broth. Can you drink it?"

"Yes, please," Magdalena sipped a little of the broth and lay back again. "What is that commotion I hear outside?"

"The men are burning Uncle Joseph's house. Papa told me we should. He also wants us to burn this house and everything in it. We can live in Papa Zeno's forge or Uncle Joseph's barn until we can build a new one. Papa says it will kill the disease."

"Yes, I believe you. You are such a blessing to us all, Daughter. Are you feeling ill at all?"

"No, Mama. I will be fine. Papa says so. Here, have some more broth. It will make you strong again."

In a few days, when she was stronger, Magdalena asked for pen and vellum to write Jude the news of the deaths. She sent Zeno to take it to the inn so Jaffrez could put it on the next boat to the harbor. When Zeno returned, he brought her a letter that had just arrived. When she opened it, she saw that it was from Nicodemus, not from Jude. Abrupt with bad news, the letter made her heart beat fast.

Magdalena:
Spies intercepted letters and know where you are.
Peter sending assassins, leaving now. God save you all.
Nicodemus.

She read it out to Zeno.

"What shall we do?"

"If the killers left at the same time as this letter, they could be here now. Go to Joseph's barn. I will go ask Jaffrez if he has seen any suspicious newcomers."

Just then, Eroica entered.

"Papa Zeno, you are not supposed to be in this house." Then, assessing the situation, she said, "What's wrong?"

"Take your mother to Joseph's barn and call in the fiercest of the dogs. I will return as soon as I can. Here, take my dagger; my sword's too big for you."

The girl did as she was told, sensing the urgency. She helped Magdalena up from her bed and walked her to the barn, which lay across two big fields. The shepherds and the dogs came to meet them. One of the men lifted and carried Magdalena, who was still too weak to walk that distance.

"Why is the youngster carrying a knife?" he asked.

"Assassins are coming for us," Magdalena said. "We don't know who they are, what they look like, or even if they are here yet. We need to hide or flee."

Suddenly, the vision from her fever dream flashed on her memory. Yeshua had told her to flee to the west. But she was too weak, and there was no time to arrange it, if the killers were at hand.

"Mama, we must pray. Now." Eroica drove the dogs out of the barn along with the men, and she sat in silence with her mother. They stilled themselves as best they could and waited to hear something. Their agitated hearts drowned out God's voice for many minutes. Calm came eventually, and Magdalena saw herself and Eroica opening the trap door atop the Tor and going in, shutting the door after them. She opened her eyes to find Eroica, open-eyed, staring at her.

"Mama, I saw the Tor."

"So did I."

"You are too weak to climb the Tor. It would be better if you swam in through the red spring."

"Daughter, you know I cannot swim."

"Then, I will bring a horse. We must leave now." And Eroica ran to one of the men, asking him to bring a bridled horse. She gathered several horse blankets from the barn and rolled them up. "When Zeno comes, tell him to put jars of food by the red spring." The men helped Magdalena to mount with Eroica in front, holding the reins, the bedroll wedged between them. "I will send the horse back down. If he doesn't arrive, you can send someone for him." Fog surrounded the Tor, shrouding the two riders from view. Magdalena was sure Yeshua had sent it to protect his widow and daughter, and she thanked him in her heart. Up the spiraling path they went till they reached the top.

"Thank you, Papa, for the fog," Eroica said. She walked straight to the secret stair and pried up the door. "Hurry, Mama. We will sleep with the old king tonight."

Magdalena carried the bedroll to the hole and stepped down in. Eroica slapped the horse on the rump and sent it off. The thud of the trap door sealed the two in darkness, until the sparkles from Eroica's hand lit the way down the stairs.

"Here, Mama, I will make our beds over here. You just lie down and rest. Oh, look, an old skull cup we can fetch some water in. I will go down to the spring. Maybe Papa Zeno will be there." And she disappeared, leaving her mother to sit in darkness with the bones of a king. Patiently she waited, knowing she was protected and loved.

When Eroica returned, soaking wet but cheerful, she

brought light and water into the burial chamber.

"I washed the skull out as much as I could. Here is some water. It's pretty rusty, but it will do you good. I carved some runes into a branch and left it outside by the spring. It said we are safe---bring food and candles. I don't know if he will find it today, but I will go down and check after a while."

"That was clever, Daughter. The assassins can't read runes, even if they found them. Here, wrap this around you. You have saved us again, you and your Papa."

"That's what Papa lived for, and that's my mission, too. Saving people, and dogs, and everything! Let's see if they buried this old king with anything useful. We can make a fire of this burial wagon if we need to, but the smoke might give us away."

"I am warm enough. We are buried deep underground, snug as a rabbit in its den."

"Here are some blankets, pretty dusty and smelly. I guess we could put them on the floor to lie on. Oh, look, another cup. Looks like this one's tin. This keg might have mead in it, if I could just open it."

"I don't think we should eat or drink anything buried here."

"All right, Mama. We will wait for Papa Zeno. Shall we sing some hymns to God?"

"I think not. Our voices might carry up the stairs or out through the spring. Maybe you could go check for Zeno again."

"Yes, Mama. I'll be right back."

When the girl returned, sprinkling light before her, she carried a bag slung over her shoulder and a small branch in her hand.

"Here's a rune message from Papa Zeno, some candles, some bread, and some apples. We can have a feast!"

"What does the message say?"

"It says...*Stay put. No sign yet. More tomorrow*. More what tomorrow? More food, more news?"

"No matter. We can rest here safe. Come here and let me cradle you like when you were little."

"Oh, Mama, I'm a big girl now."

"I know you are, but I am not. I still need cuddles to make me feel loved."

"All right, Mama. If it makes you feel stronger, I will hold you." And the two rested in each other's arms. They had no sense of time's passing, locked as they were away from the sun and moon. Still, they were alive and they were safe, for the time being.

Chapter 21

Flight

They awoke when the barking of dogs rose up the staircase from the spring below. Eroica descended, slipped into the underground pool, and emerged cautiously at the spring, among the ferns. There stood Zeno with two dogs on leads.

"Hello, Eroica," he said in a soft voice. "I have news. Here is another bag of food and a sword. The assassins arrived yesterday, posing as wine traders from Greece. They are at the inn. They have been asking around and walking the town. King Arveragus has put his army on alert, and we meet today to plan strategy. We are trying to find out if the two at the inn have brought reinforcements. Your friend Alby has tethered a coracle in the marsh where this spring flows into it. You and your mother may have to take it downstream, preferably at night. Have you ever managed a coracle?"

"I went out with Alby one time, but he steered. I

have no skill."

"Well, that may not be necessary. So far, the spies haven't paid any attention to the Tor. They asked about it, but Jaffrez told them it was just a mound with a flat top, nowhere to hide. How is your mother?"

"She is resting and growing stronger. When will you come again?"

"I can't say for sure. I will come once a day, or I will send Alby. You must have heard the dogs barking."

"Yes, Mama said we couldn't sing because folks might hear. I guess she was right. The dogs' voices floated right up like smoke in a chimney."

"Right. Listen for the dogs. That will be our signal. Stay quiet, stay safe. I will be back." Zeno left, and Eroica took her mother breakfast.

Using the dagger, Eroica spent the hours carving runes on the wood of the burial wagon. Names of all her friends and family, the names of the dogs, and some prayers made up the text. She taught the fundamentals to her mother who found it took her mind off her worries. If she and her daughter died at the hands of assassins, at least they would die together and they would be reunited with God.

Not barking but the sound of men's voices above them woke Magdalena and Eroica. Scraping of metal tools told them that someone was prying open the trap door at the staircase top.

"Mama, we must go."

"Where?"

"Down. To the coracle. Come!" And Eroica took her mother by the hand and urged her down the steps. When they reached the dark, silent pool, Magdalena hesitated.

"But Daughter, I am afraid."

"I know, Mama, but you can do this. Just hold your breath and put your arms around my waist. We will only be under water for a short time, and we will pop up at the red spring. Here we go." Eroica with her mother in tow dived under the water's black surface and swam toward the opening, in the direction of the sound of trickling water. Magdalena held her breath and closed her eyes. She clung to her girl and instinctively kicked her feet to help move them along. When her head came above water, she still saw darkness, but there were stars twinkling in it. Wet and shivering, they stood outside in the fresh air.

"Grab them. There they are!" a rough voice shouted nearby, and Magdalena felt strong arms pin her in a tight grip.

Eroica screamed and started kicking and scratching at the man who had caught her. Nearby stood two other men, with torches, looking on. In the distance, barking dogs yelped as they ran toward the spring. The girl's screams drowned out the barking so that the assassins were startled by the arrival of the dogs and the men who ran in with them.

In the torchlight, Magdalena made out Zeno's face wearing the most warlike expression she had ever seen. With him were the king's sons Alan and Brennus. They said nothing, just attacked the men with swords and battle axes. When the assassins dropped their captives to defend themselves, Magdalena and Eroica ran to take cover in the trees, far away from the bloodshed.

"Mama, should we run? What if the assassins kill Zeno and the soldiers?"

Magdalena put her arm around Eroica. "They won't. I have a feeling."

Metal clanked on metal, torchlight glinted off of

blades, men groaned and panted, bodies thudded to the ground. When the fighting stopped, Zeno came with a torch to find his family.

"You can come out now. Are you all right?"

"Yes, are you?"

"Fine. I haven't fought like that since I was a young man. It feels good."

Magdalena noticed that Zeno had a cut on his cheek, but she knew just the remedy for that.

"Let me see these men," Magdalena said.

Zeno brought the torch close enough for her to see. She took in her breath.

"That looks like Barabbas. He's come all these miles after all these years? Does evil have no bounds?"

"Mama, how can you say that? Yes, these men are the bounds," Eroica said, gesturing toward the standing men. "They saved us. We are very grateful, sirs."

"Yes, I am forgetting myself. We are very grateful."

Just then, horses and men with more torches approached, having descended the path from the Tor. Among them were King Arveragus and his other son, Eppenos. Slung over the backs of the horses were the dead bodies of three other assassins, the ones who had opened the trap door.

"You were right to leave when you did. These cutthroats would have gutted you both in a second," Eppenos said.

"We heard them breaking in the door, so we went down and out through the spring," Eroica explained.

"You mean your mother swam?" Zeno asked, incredulous.

"Yes, I did. Underwater, too. And I'm freezing."

This sparked action in the king's gallant sons, and two of them offered their cloaks to warm the woman and the girl. Eroica, on the cusp of womanhood, blushed at the handsome Brennus's attentions. Magdalena noticed, as did Zeno.

"Thank you very much," Eroica breathed, smiling at the prince.

"I am happy to serve you, my lady."

"We had better go home to our beds," Zeno said.

"I believe your house has been burned. You will be my guests tonight, and my wife and daughters will tend to the wounds you have suffered in this cause," Arveragus said. No one argued with him.

———————————— • ————————————

Around the king's sumptuous breakfast table the next day, the participants recounted the previous day's events in vivid detail to Queen Alys and her daughters. Stories, legends, and epic poems seemed to come easily to the natives of Britannia, and listening to such tales gave much pleasure. Arveragus narrated the main events, with his sons adding their own details and perspectives. As she listened, Eroica fell more and more in love with Brennus. When the story-telling was done, the problem-solving began. What should be done now? Of course, the criminals should be buried and forgotten. But would not others come in their wake? Was it safe to remain in Glastonbury?

A servant broke into the discussion with an urgent letter sent on by Jaffrez at the inn. It was directed to the king. As Arveragus read it, his face clouded. More bad news.

"This may have some bearing on your decision, my friends. My spies report that the Romans are mustering a large force of three divisions in Gaul, in preparation for invasion."

"But we already have tribute arrangements with the Romans," Eppenos said.

"Yes, but that's not enough for them. Their empire doesn't run on an empty stomach---or on an empty purse. This is going to be a real war. We will all have to fight or flee."

Magdalena felt a cold thrill down her neck. Fight or flee. Should she tell of the message she had heard?

"If I may, I will share a word I heard from my husband Yeshua, the prophet. He said to me: 'Run away to the west. Don't fight them.' I thought he meant the assassins, but perhaps he meant the Romans," Magdalena said.

Arveragus's solemn look said that her input was unwelcome. "We are a fighting people. We don't run from aggressors. Besides, this is our land, and we will defend it to the death."

"I'm sorry. I didn't mean to offend. I just thought you should know."

"Husband, maybe we should listen to Magdalena. We are a fighting people, but we are also a peaceful people at heart. We have cousins in Anglesey. Perhaps we could go west to live with them."

"And do you think the Romans will stop at Anglesey? I say we make a stand here, in our homeland, not run away to hide in the west."

No one dared to contradict Arveragus. The power and the tradition of his long ancestry supported him. He valued courage more than survival. Never mind what women, Druids, and foreign prophets said.

Zeno broached another topic. "Sir, we are so grateful for the gift of land you gave to Joseph and to Magdalena. If we decide to move west ahead of the Romans, we would like to give you back the land. After all, it is part of your realm. The only part we would ask be preserved is the chapel."

Magdalena looked at Zeno. They had not discussed any of this. It was her land and her chapel. However, she saw that Zeno, always the clever manager, had a plan in mind, so she tamed her tongue.

The king replied, "Nonsense, that land is yours to sell or trade. If you intend to sell, I will give you a good price for it. Of course we will preserve the chapel. It's a monument to your ancestors, Joseph and Mary. There may even be some in Glastonbury who could keep teaching your ideas there. I hear you have a goodly number of followers."

"Yes, we have," Magdalena said. "We would be very grateful if people remembered Yeshua here. He wanted us to spread his words all over the world. This may be the farthest west they ever reach."

"Perhaps that is why you are so concerned for your safety. You are trying to preserve a tradition."

"It is a very new tradition, one that has barely gotten a foothold. If the Romans wipe us out, that will be the end of Yeshua's wisdom."

"We can't have that," the king said. "The university will remember him, and I will take responsibility for keeping the chapel repaired. I promise you."

"God bless you, sir," Magdalena said.

"You needn't be gone. You are welcome to stay here as long as it takes to decide whether you wish to rebuild your house or move west," Arveragus said. Queen Alys smiled her agreement.

"Thank you for your kindness, my lord," Magdalena said. "I see the west beckoning to us."

"If you will let me," Queen Alys said, "I will give you the direction of my cousins in Anglesey, should you need their help."

"I am grateful. Thank you," Magdalena said, and the three departed.

Chapter 22

Ynis Enlli

Nevanthi, Magdalena, and Eroica bent over the workbench in Nevanthi's shed. They were picking over herbs, tinctures, and ointments that the travelers might need on their journey or at their new home. If Magdalena needed to earn a living, she could set up as a healer with all the medicines Nevanthi gave her.

"You know, you should take some seeds as well. You might need to plant a garden to feed yourselves. They take little space in your bags, and they are life-savers," Nevanthi advised.

"We will need an oak tree to pray under, and apples to eat. I will take some acorns and apples," Eroica said.

"I wish we could take sheep seeds and cow seeds. We don't plan to herd our livestock along with us. We want to travel quietly and swiftly. Arveragus is buying the stock along with the land."

"Then you will have the money to buy a new farm

and new livestock wherever you settle. I will miss you all, but I wish you well. If we need to escape the Romans, perhaps we will see you again some day," Nevanthi said, embracing her friends.

The next day, after bidding the royal family farewell, they set off on horse back. Eroica rode her own mount. Each of the three horses carried packs, including Zeno's tools and Magdalena's herbs, but they owned very little since their house had been burned. On the way through town, they stopped at the inn to say good-bye to Kwyn and Jaffrez, who gave them food to carry with them. Magdalena promised to write to Kwyn, as soon as she knew where she would be living. Kwyn cried at the loss of her friends, expecting never to meet them again.

Zeno and Jaffrez had planned the route, and the riders set off to the northwest, hoping to reach the sea in about twenty miles. Camping for the night on the beach by the great Severn estuary, they looked over the dark water and breathed the salt air.

"Mama, it reminds me of the smell of our home in Caesarea," Eroica said.

"Do you remember that smell?"

"Of course I do! I remember Papa Zeno teaching me to swim, and escaping the bad men in the little boat, with the dolphins. I remember everything. Mama, will we have to run from bad men forever?" Eroica asked.

Magdalena, taken aback, didn't answer at first. She hadn't realized that Eroica saw her life as one fearful flight from enemies. The girl's peace had wavered precariously all her life long.

"No, my daughter, we will find peace and safety in our new home."

"How do you know?"

Again, she couldn't answer.

"We will keep moving till we find it."

Eroica sighed. Her mother's words which had always reassured her in the past seemed to have lost their power and trustworthiness. Zeno intervened.

"Remember, Eroica, we are not just trying to save our own skins. We want to keep your father's teachings alive. If we die, his ideas die with us."

"What about my Papa's other followers? They are still alive, aren't they? That man Paul and Nicodemus and Martha and Mary. They are teachers too."

"Yes, they are. And now, I think we need to sleep. Tomorrow, we will reach the city of Abona where we can board a ship to Anglesey," Zeno said.

Eroica subsided. Why did adults not make as much sense as they used to? She would ask her papa in heaven.

Sleeping uncomfortably on the ground, all three of the family had dreams and broken sleep. When they woke with the sun, they ate a small meal and spoke of their dreams.

"I saw a woman who looked like Nevanthi. She kept shaking her head and saying, 'Not Anglesey. Not Anglesey,'" Magdalena said.

"I saw a bloody battle between a Roman division and the poor, local people. Nobody told me, but I knew it was Anglesey," Zeno said.

"I saw my papa writing with a stick on the sand. He wrote words I don't know: Y-N-I-S E-N-L-L-I. What does that mean?" Eroica asked.

"I guess we are not meant to go to Anglesey, but I have never heard of Ynis Enlli," Magdalena said. "We should continue on to Abona. One of the ship captains will surely know. We must thank God for the messages."

"Thank you, God," Zeno said.

"Yes, thank you, Papa," Eroica said.

At the bustling dock in Abona, where the rivers Avon and Severn flowed into the wide estuary that led to the Irish Sea, Zeno inquired around until he found a ship that called in at ports along the Welsh coast.

"Captain, we would like to book passage for the three of us and perhaps our horses, to a place called Ynis Enlli," Zeno said.

"Ha! Surely not. Nobody goes to that god-forsaken island. It's hard to reach and damn-all when you get there. Who told you to go there?" the captain scoffed.

"God did," Magdalena said.

The captain's eyes widened. He had met lots of crazy religious zealots in his time, and he thought best to humor them, especially if it meant a lucrative fare.

"Well, I can place you on Ynis Enlli, but there is no harbor, so you will have to be rowed ashore in a boat. That means the horses can't go. And you better buy some woolen blankets and cloaks. The wind whips across that place like a banshee. It will cost you---" and the captain named an exorbitant fare which the sale of the horses would barely cover.

"Fine," Magdalena said. "When do we sail?"

"Tomorrow at daybreak, when the tide is high enough to clear the estuary. By the time we reach the island, the tide should be lower, giving you a wider beach to land on. There's the ship, the *Salmon*," the captain said, pointing to the ship at dock.

"And where might we sell our horses?"

"The proprietor of the Ship might buy them, or the smith on the quay. They look like fine animals. Don't take less than two staters for them," and the captain strode up the plank to his vessel, leaving them to find their way to the Ship inn.

The owner of the Ship inn took the horses for the

equivalent of the fare plus one night's lodging for three, with supper. At dawn, the small family boarded the *Salmon* and sailed out of the estuary into the rough waters of the Irish Sea, very different from the smooth, blue Mediterranean. Eroica still spoke to the sea birds and dolphins she saw, but not with the vivacity and joy of her childhood self. Dark thoughts stopped the flow of her usual energy, and her mother and Zeno noticed it.

In late afternoon, the island appeared in golden light shining from the west onto the flat land that rose to a rocky hill in the east.

"Is that it? No wonder the captain said what he did," Zeno said.

"Good for planting and sheep. It's not far to the mainland," Magdalena said, trying to be positive.

"But there are no trees. None at all. How long does an oak take to grow? I brought a dozen acorns and lots of apples," Eroica said.

"They take a long time."

"Then I better plant as soon as we land," Eroica said, taking her mother's arm.

The captain interrupted.

"This is as far as we can take the ship. Bundle yourselves into that boat, and my men will row you ashore. There are a few families of farmers and fishermen who live on the island. I hear they are friendly. Good luck to you three. I will say a prayer each time I pass by in the *Salmon*."

"Thank you, Captain. May God bless you," Magdalena said. The captain nodded and took his leave.

"For Grandmary's sake, I am glad she is not here today. She would not like stepping into this boat," Eroica said.

"I don't like it much myself," Magdalena huffed.

"Don't be scared, Mama. You know I will keep us all safe."

The sailors drove the boat as far up the shingle beach as they could, then stepped out into the water to pull it in farther. They took the bundles Zeno and Magdalena handed them and assisted the women to disembark. There was no help for it; feet and hems were wet and cold as they trudged up the slope to the flat grassland of the island. Wind swept relentlessly across the meadow, and no dwellings appeared.

"If there are any people on this barren scrap, they must be sheltering in the lea of the hill," Zeno said. "Let's head that way." All three carried their baggage and pushed ahead, leaning into the wind. Before long, the wind brought them the sound of a dog's barking, angry and urgent.

"Well, somebody lives here," Magdalena said. "From the sound of that dog, they don't like strangers."

"Never mind, Mama. The dog will like me," Eroica said, striding forward to be the first to meet the dog. She was a large, long-haired, scraggly beast, baring her fangs and barking from deep in her chest. Eroica bravely approached the dog, speaking in her animal-calming voice. Two more barks, and the dog was sniffing the girl's hand, then submitting to be stroked between the ears. "See, Mama, this sweet dog is a long-time friend of mine. She knows me well." The dog fell in beside Eroica and accompanied the family to her farmstead, just hidden over a rise. Her people lived in a small stone cottage, and the sheep and goats had a barn. The dog lived where she chose.

Zeno called a greeting in the language of his former neighbors in Glastonbury, hoping he might be understood. The dog punctuated it with a few barks. Out

from the barn, rake in hand, came the farmer, looking
suspicious. He saw that Eroica had charmed his dog, and
that eased him a bit.

"Welcome," the farmer said without enthusiasm.
"Come to the house. Marvina, we have company," he
called to his wife.

"Company? Is it Alma?" When she opened the
door, she stepped back in surprise to see three soggy,
windblown strangers. "Oh, my. Company indeed. Come
in and warm yourselves by the fire. I will make you some
tea. I am Marvina, and my husband is Kelven."

"Please, what is the dog called?" Eroica asked.

"She is Ula. We gave her a tree name to make us think
of all the trees we don't have. Ula means elm. And what
are your names?"

Zeno introduced himself and the women, as is
traditional for the man of the household. Kelven and
Marvina took him to be the husband of Magdalena and
father of Eroica, and for the time being that was fine. No
need to complicate their story. As Marvina poured out a
tea brewed from local herbs, Magdalena and Zeno took
turns sharing their story.

"So, the gods showed you a vision to bring you here?"
Kelven asked.

"Yes, we were headed to Anglesey, but God warned us
to come here instead. We both have skills to share with
the community. I work all metals, and Magdalena is a
healer."

"A healer and a wise woman, I wager," Marvina
said. "That is why the gods sent you. Our wise woman,
Rhonwen, died recently. She was a hundred years old.
You were sent to take her place."

Magdalena smiled. She felt the warmth of welcome
flowing from Marvina's countenance, and took her rough

217

hand.

"I would be honored to help," Magdalena said. "My daughter is something of a healer herself, and she has a way with animals."

"Wonderful!" Marvina took Kelven aside after slicing some bread for the visitors. She returned smiling. "Perhaps young Nyal would let you have his grandmother's cottage. He lives with the fisher family now. You need a place to stay, and winter is no time to build."

"We sold our own farm in Glastonbury, so we can pay him for the cottage," Zeno said.

"That will suit him, I think. He's of the age when young men think of marrying, and he is saving up what he earns for that future event. You will sleep here tonight, and we can approach Nyal in the morning," Kelven said.

Marvina gave Magdalena and Eroica the only bed while the others bedded down where they could, near the fireplace.

In their bed, Eroica whispered to her mother, "See, Mama, Papa is keeping us safe and sending us new friends. Tomorrow we will see our new home." Magdalena kissed her girl and cuddled her close for warmth. Ynis Enlli island was the coldest place she had ever slept.

Chapter 23

Village

After a breakfast of cheese and bread, Kelven and Marvina took the newcomers to meet the village. Only about thirty people lived on the island, some farmers and some fishermen, and their families. The cottage in question was built of stone quarried from the hill. It had two rooms, one for sleeping and the other for cooking and living. The small windows on the lea side had wooden shutters to keep out the wind. Magdalena saw that Rhonwen's kitchen was well supplied with shelves and hooks for storing herbs and tinctures, and some of her medicines still remained. A table and two stools, a bedstead, and a cooking pot hanging in the fireplace were the only other furnishings. The small shed behind the house might be expanded into a forge for Zeno. The house suited them well.

"When will we be able to talk to Nyal?" Magdalena said.

"You can talk to him now," a young man said, ducking his head under the lintel of the door. "I am Nyal."

Magdalena thought she could hear Eroica's heart stop beating as she looked at the handsome young stranger. She knew her daughter had felt the first stirrings of love around Brennus, King Arveragus's son, and she was not surprised to see her eyes take on that shine that comes at first encounter with the one. Eroica, almost twelve, was ripe to fall in love with a man a few years her senior, with dark, shaggy hair and tall stature. Though she was not surprised by the fact of Eroica's falling, she was surprised at the fear that stirred within her. Protective motherhood reared its head, and Magdalena looked at Nyal with suspicion.

Kelven introduced the parties, and Nyal immediately agreed terms with Zeno to rent the cottage for a monthly fee.

"You can move in today, if you like. I will bring you a load of peat for the fire," Nyal said.

"And here are two loaves of bread."

"And a flagon of beer."

"And some cheese."

All these voices came from villagers gathered outside the door to welcome the newcomers. It wasn't every day that a wise woman and a smith moved into the village on Ynis Enlli. Everyone wanted a look at the new arrivals, and they couldn't arrive empty-handed.

"Is there a shop to buy supplies on the island?" Magdalena asked, though she had seen all of the village on her tour and knew there was no shop.

"No, but I take my boat to the mainland once a week and bring goods back," Nyal said. "Then we have a sort of market down on the dock. If you need any particular thing, let me know and I will try to get it for you. As you see, we have no cattle on the island, and no trees, so cow's milk and apples have to come from the mainland, as well as wood for building. I hope you like fish, because there's plenty of them."

Zeno smiled at Nyal. He seemed an enterprising young fisherman, also managing a weekly market for the island's residents.

"Nyal, do you also take passengers across? I will need to lay in goods for my forge, and I wouldn't want to burden you with the details of my needs."

"Yes, but the more passengers, the less goods I can bring back. Have you ever fished?"

Zeno shook his head. "No, but I'm willing to learn, if that would help you."

"Yes, if we bring in a good catch, we take it to the mainland fish market, unload it, and there will be plenty of space for your metals and such. A combined trip."

"You have a deal."

"May I come along? I am very good at fishing," Eroica said, beaming at Nyal.

The young man looked at her for the first time. He had passed her over as a child, but now he registered her shining eyes and knew that though she was young, she was remarkable.

"Are you now?" Nyal said, smiling.

"Well, I have never really caught any, but they speak to me and I know how to call them."

"Really? They come to you when you call?"

Eroica all of a sudden felt the eyes of everyone on her, and she blushed. This was a new feeling for her. Where had her innocent bravery gone? She had never been cowed like this before.

"Yes," she whispered, looked down, and withdrew from the limelight. Magdalena noticed the change in her

221

daughter, and her fear swelled. No longer a girl, Eroica had embarked on womanhood with all its pains and uncertainties. Magdalena thought it was too soon. She needed to pray, but there were no trees to sit under, neither olive nor oak.

———————— • ● • ————————

Sweeping out the cottage, bringing their few belongings from Kelven's farm, making the bed, and clearing out the shed kept the family busy for a few days. Zeno found a box in the shed to use for a third stool until he could make better seats. Neighbors brought more food, and her first patient came in for medicine. It was Beatha, an old woman, stooped over with age.

"Hello," she called at the door, "is the healer at home?"

"Yes," Magdalena said, "come in. How can I help?"

"Rhonwen used to give me a syrup for the pains in my legs. I wonder if you have any of that."

"I can make you some willow bark tea. Have a seat. My name is Magdalena."

"I am Beatha. If you can help the pains of old age, you will have lots of customers. Nobody dies on this island until late in life. I will be a hundred next month, just like Rhonwen. We were girls together."

"Really? Why do you think folks live so long?" Magdalena asked as she got the bark ready to steep.

"The gods know, I don't. The plagues and fevers don't seem to jump over the two miles of water that separate us from the mainland. We are lucky that way. If you all came from Palestine, are you worshipers of Yahweh? We have never had any Yahweh people on the island. We sacrifice to the old gods."

"Yes, we have only the one god, Yahweh. But we

learned of all the old gods in Glastonbury when we lived there."

"Does Yahweh make your healing more powerful?"

"I think so, because he built all the healing into the herbs I use. I pray, too. It's a mystery how it all works. What do you think?"

"I think all the gods, including yours, want us to live as long as we can and spend all that time loving each other. So, whatever keeps us alive and loving, that is the good," Beatha said, sipping her tea.

"And I think you have loved many people in your hundred years," Magdalena said.

"Yes and no. In my early years I was full of anger and fear. I kept myself away from people. I only loved the sky and the sea. I sat on the shore all day, dreaming of seeing the big world. My mother would scream at me to come in and do my chores. I ignored her until she came after me with a strap. I am sorry for all the pain I caused her. I didn't start loving until I was a grown woman and had my own children. I never belted them. I always talked to them as you talk to grown folks, like you do with your daughter."

Magdalena looked surprised; she had just met Beatha. How did she know her manner with Eroica?

Beatha said, "Don't worry. I have been around when you and your girl are out foraging and talking. There is a special light about her, isn't there?"

"Yes, her father was a prophet."

"And a healer?"

"Yes, a great healer." Magdalena's voice broke as she spoke. Since she left Glastonbury, she had not communicated with Yeshua. Her heart ached.

"Something is weighing upon you, my dear. I see the signs. There is a path that winds almost to the top of the hill. On a still day, you might climb up there to talk to your god or your prophet. I know Rhonwen swore by it, when she needed divine strength. Thank you for the tea, Magdalena. I hope we will be fast friends."

"We will, Beatha. Here is more bark for you to take home with you. Peace be with you."

Beatha caressed Magdalena's face with her gnarled hand and left the cottage. Magdalena pushed back the shutter to look up at the hill, but the wind blew it back in her face. Today was not the day to climb the hill.

When Zeno returned from his first fishing trip, he and Nyal pushed a hand cart up from the dock, laden with goods. Zeno had purchased metals and a new bellows for his forge, as well as wood for building. In wooden tubs, three sapling trees wobbled in the cart, a gift for Eroica from Nyal: an oak, an apple, and a walnut tree.

When Eroica saw the trees Nyal had brought her, she threw her arms around him and embraced him joyfully. Magdalena frowned.

"Oh, thank you so much, Nyal. I will take such good care of them, they will grow where no tree has ever grown. And you shall eat the first apple that ripens, I promise."

Nyal smiled at that, and Magdalena wondered if he read the underlying implication of the girl's words. Zeno definitely did, and looked at Magdalena's frown. Young Nyal would have a formidable adversary in Eroica's mother.

Rather than ask Magdalena's permission, Nyal spoke to Eroica in secret about a boat trip to see the dolphins and seals. She agreed without hesitation since she had no fear of water, the ocean, or boats.

Magdalena noticed none of the clues Eroica gave that something was in the offing. She was too preoccupied with the heaviness in her spirit that Beatha had remarked on. She felt foggy, stupefied, sluggish. She had no sense of God's presence, no messages from Yeshua, no waves of energy coming to her from any source. She had to climb the hill.

The gods must have heard her prayer, for the day dawned calm and cloudy. Magdalena set off to climb the hill, so focused that she paid no attention to where Eroica was. The girl was boarding Nyal's boat at the dock while her mother climbed the rocky trail up the landward side of the hill that formed the bulwark protecting Ynis Enlli. The trail ended near the top where solid rock formed the skullcap of the hill. Magdalena found a seat in a crevice, and tried to still her mind for prayer. After several minutes, unable to enter that holy place, she opened her eyes and looked across the gray sea. A slight breeze brought her the sound of her daughter's voice, laughing in a boat on the water. A pod of four dolphins leapt above the water and dived in again. Eroica laughed again, and Magdalena felt anger mounting within her. Nyal had taken her daughter on the sea without asking. Her daughter had deceived her, gone behind her back. She would put a stop to it! She rose abruptly, and slipped on the rocky path, falling hard on her hip. A pain shot up her side and down her leg. What now? She had no way to call for help. She had not told Zeno where she was going, eager as she was to talk to Yeshua. She lay still, and breathed in, directing her breath to the painful spot on her hip. Some relief came. She waited, breathing, until she thought she could walk, and she slowly descended the path. Her anger had gotten the best of her, she realized, but she still wanted to put an end to Eroica's romance.

Chapter 24

Break

Magdalena waited, fuming, for Eroica to return to the cottage. She had not felt this angry since before she met Yeshua---back when she was married to Tiras. Part of her heart sensed the encroachment of her old demons, but she refused to admit them to her conscious mind. Pacing back and forth in the kitchen, she rehearsed the words she would use to attack Nyal and her daughter.

Zeno entered before the lovers, and he saw Magdalena's dark looks.

"My lady, can I help you in any way?"

"Have you got a sharpened blade I can use on that boy?"

"Surely you are joking, Magdalena," Zeno said. Just then, Eroica and Nyal arrived, laughing and walking an arm's length apart, trying to look innocent, as Magdalena thought.

"And where have you two been?"

"Collecting samphire on the sea rocks," Eroica lied.

"Really? Where is it?"

"We dropped it off at Beatha's. She loves it."

"Liar! I saw you from the hill. The two of you took a boat out without asking my permission."

Eroica and Nyal looked abashed and said nothing.

Magdalena continued, stoking the fire, "Do you deny it? Will you pile more lies on the first?"

"No, Mama. I don't deny it. We didn't ask because you would have said no."

"You're right about that, little hussy! You are not to see this scoundrel any more, do you hear me? I will tie you up if I have to. This sneaking affair ends here. Nyal, go home. I never want to see your face again. Eroica, go in the sleeping room and think about what you have become, a liar and a sneak." The two young people did as they were told. With her face red, and her heart pounding, Magdalena had to breathe the air. She headed toward Kelven's farm, with Zeno following at a distance. He hadn't seen her in such a state for years, and he knew what she was capable of when under the control of her demons. He followed her past the farm and over to the shingle beach where they had landed from the *Salmon*.

Magdalena paced up and down the bluff above the beach, kicking at clumps of grass and tearing her hair. Finally, she sat down on the bluff and put her head in her hands. Zeno waited to see if she would erupt again, but she stayed still. He approached slowly.

"My lady, I am here," he said.

"Oh, Zeno. I am in darkness. Yeshua has left me. He said our love would last across time and space, but now he is gone. I can't reach him any more." Deep sobs wracked her body, and the tears bleared her face.

"I think that is not possible. Yeshua is always with you, but the demons have come upon you again, for some reason."

"No, he has abandoned me. No dreams, no messages, no presence. Nothing but darkness. I am lost." She indulged in more sobs.

"My lady, when Yeshua helped you to drive out the demons, back in the wilderness, remember---what did he have you do?"

"I don't remember. I don't want to think about it. It's too painful."

"But you must. You can't let them win. Please, my lady, for Eroica's sake, for my sake..."

"Eroica. What has happened to her? She defies me, she sneaks behind my back, she carries on with some young rascal. Where is my blessed daughter?" She let out a frustrated moan that burned her throat.

Zeno looked at Magdalena, letting the silence answer her brainless question. She saw the answer hanging in the air, but refused it.

"I see you are saying that she is growing up. Must growing up always contain so much pain and deceit? She is a special girl, a magical girl. She should be beyond such adolescent shenanigans."

"My lady, she is a human girl like any other. Her heart wants what everyone wants, and Nyal is a fine young man, I think. I like him."

Magdalena didn't want to hear anything about that young man, the predator whose mouth was watering over the innocent body of her child. It was too much.

"Zeno, did we manage to salvage any of the blue water lily I had?"

Zeno's face paled. When Magdalena went for the

blue water lily, she was spiraling down into the depths. She would drink and drug herself into oblivion, maybe to death if he let her.

"No, my lady. It was all gone before we left Glastonbury. We only have some beer, but I saw some Greek wine in the market. I will buy you some on my next trip to the mainland."

"With that evil Nyal? No, I want to have nothing to do with him."

"But, Magdalena, we live on a tiny island with him. He is our neighbor. We can't avoid him forever. We depend on him for fish and other supplies. Be reasonable."

"Oh, Zeno! How about poppy? Did Nevanthi send us with any poppy?"

"I don't know. Let's go home and see. Come, my lady. It's growing windy and cold," and Zeno helped Magdalena up from the sandy bluff. They walked back to the cottage, Magdalena intending to kill her pain with medicine of some kind, and Zeno intending to hide the poppy if he could find it.

When they entered the cottage, Eroica was gone. Magdalena threw herself onto the bed in a fit of anger and despair.

"I will go find her, my lady. She probably went to Beatha for comfort," Zeno said softly.

"Beatha! Ha! She will be screwing Nyal in his boat on the dock! Tell her she can do what she wants, but she is no longer my daughter. Cut off. Out of my house. She can go with Nyal, and good luck to her. Tell her that!" and she buried her head in the covers.

Zeno breathed a deep sigh and left the house. He found Eroica at Beatha's tiny cot, with red eyes, sipping from a cup of broth. The three stayed together, talking over Magdalena's state, until well after dark.

"The girl is welcome to stay here tonight," Beatha said. "I would be glad of the company."

"I'd like to stay with Beatha, and maybe my mother will be calmer tomorrow. I will talk to my Papa in heaven. He will tell me what I can do to help her," Eroica said. Zeno nodded and returned to the cottage he shared with Magdalena. He found her asleep on her rumpled bed.

Chapter 25

Free

When Magdalena woke, the room was dark, and Eroica sat at the foot of the bed sprinkling light from her finger tips.

"Good morning, Mama," Eroica said, "I asked for Papa's help last night, and he gave me advice."

Magdalena pushed her hair back and touched her daughter's shoulder.

"How is it that he still speaks to you, but he won't speak to me?" Her voice sounded flat, hopeless.

"I asked him that. He says he is always speaking, but something is blocking you from hearing him."

"What is it?"

"He will show you. Come with me." Eroica roused her mother from the bed, wrapped a cloak around her, and walked with her from the cottage, her arm linked with Magdalena's. The sky was darkly clouded, but the wind was calm. Magdalena realized that Eroica was taking her to climb the hill, and she hesitated, not wanting to remember yesterday's climb and what she saw. "It will be fine, Mama. Trust Papa."

Eroica urged her mother to ascend first. When they reached a flat place on the path, they stopped and sat side-by-side, looking out over the gray sea. Eroica tenderly adjusted the cloak around Magdalena's shoulders.

Magdalena said, "My love, I am sorry about yesterday. I don't know what is wrong with me."

"Papa knows. Now just breathe this fresh, cool air, and close your eyes. Papa wants to show you a moving play behind your eyes. Picture the day you followed him from the river to the cave. See the place, who you were with, and how you felt." Eroica paused to give her mother time. "How did you feel, Mama?"

"I felt excited and brave. I knew what I was doing was the right thing."

"Now, picture the night you poured oil on Papa's hair, at the Passover dinner. How did you feel?"

"I felt like my heart was breaking, but I felt strong. I was not afraid of what the others thought. I did what I meant to do."

"Good. Now picture the day that Papa was killed." Magdalena flinched. "Can you tell me how you felt?"

"I was empty. I was lost. But I was determined to stay there. I felt love like a strong force, holding me up and binding me to your Papa. And I kept that feeling all through the night at the tomb and when I saw him in the morning."

"Were you afraid?"

"No. Not at all."

"Now, Papa wants you to take over the play. Picture the day after Papa left, when you first became afraid."

Eroica sat in silence, watching her mother's face. She saw the brow furrow, the lids twitch, the head shake. "When was it, Mama?"

"When I realized I was with child. When I realized I had someone else to protect---you."

"Yes! Now let the pictures flow from one into the next---every time you acted out of fear. From the moment you realized you needed to protect me, up to the present moment."

A cavalcade of terror flooded through Magdalena's mind's eye: strangers at the New Moon School, hiding in Caesarea, lying in the skiff under a tarp, being pulled by sea monsters, traveling through strange lands, hiding in the Tor, swimming under water, fleeing from Glastonbury, boarding a boat for unknown shores, and finally---Nyal and her daughter alone in a boat.

Magdalena dropped her face into her hands and sobbed.

"What is it, Mama?"

"I know what is blocking me from your Papa. It's fear. I was never afraid when he was with me. I was the bravest of all his disciples. He used to call me his Tower, I was so strong. But then, with him gone and you to care for, I became cowardly. I started running away. And that's when my visions stopped. I lost my ears to hear---they were stopped up with fear."

Eroica embraced her mother, and tears ran down her face.

"And your Papa taught me what to do with those forces that blocked me from God's love."

"What did he teach you, Mama?"

"To take the fears, roll them into a ball," and as she said this her hands mimed the action of rolling a ball. "Squeeze it hard, so I can feel its power and heat. Then give it to the invisible hand."

Magdalena raised her hand to the sky, holding up her compressed fears. Just then, the clouds split and a beam of sunlight arrowed down to enfold the mother and daughter. Magdalena opened her hand, and released the fear into the light stream.

"Mama, did you see that? It looked like Papa's hand taking it from you."

"Maybe. And I want to hand another burden over to him."

"What's that?"

"You, my girl. He has always kept you safe; it wasn't me. When I took over your life, I blocked out your Papa, in more ways than I knew. Oh, can you forgive me?"

"Yes, Mama," and Eroica kissed her mother's cheek. "Can we go down and tell Papa Zeno that we are friends again?"

"Yes, and will you ask young Nyal to come by? I want to ask his forgiveness, too. I was very wrong in what I said to him."

"Of course, Mama. Everything will be well, don't you think?"

"Everything will be well. God will make sure of that. It's not up to me. I am so relieved."

Eroica laughed and helped her mother up. The two women sang at the tops of their lungs all the way down the hill, not afraid to be overheard by anyone.

About this book and me, Pamella Bowen

After publishing two novels in early 2020, I was spent---no inspiration for another book, until I asked a "what if" question: What if women ran the church? Unsurprisingly, I was fed up with my church and all organized religion, including Christianity. So, I started reading about women's place in the early Christian church, which led me to Mary Magdalene, whoever she was. In summer of 2020, I jumped in and let my imagination blend scripture, apocryphal gospels, women's ancient wisdom, Celtic and Druid practices, history, and personal experiences to make this novel. It's a love story, an escape adventure, a spiritual journey, a historical romance, and a speculative fantasy all in one. Forgive me for the liberties I took with Biblical scenes and characters.

I have been writing since I retired from teaching high school English in 2009. I always wanted to write, but like most writers I had been taught that I couldn't. I had to make a living in a secure profession, they told me, so I did that for 33 years. Now, on my modest teacher pension, I have the freedom to write what I want and publish it. I started out writing country song lyrics, then Christian lyrics, poetry, children's books, devotionals, and novels. It's all been part of growing up and letting go of expectations, limits, control, and cravings.

I live happily in an empty nest with my husband Don. Our two daughters live in Nevada and Nebraska, leaving us here in Temecula, California.

Thanks for picking up this book. You have made my dream come true.

Pamella Bowen

Other Books by Pamella Bowen, available at amazon.com

For Grown-ups:

The Blindness of Odile

Labyrinth Wakening: A Spiritual Journey Novel

Destiny Fair

Bombs, Betty, and Bed-counts: A Memoir of WWII and Beyond

A Doubter's Devotional, 1&2

Play to God: Rediscover Childlike Joy

For Children:

Folding Memory: An Alzheimer's story

Faith and Grace Say Their Prayers

Faith and Grace: Puppy Love

Faith and Grace Go Birding (coming soon)

Old Vine and Little Branch

Vid Viejo y Ramita

Pray for the World

www.ingramcontent.com/pod-product-compliance
Lightning Source LLC
Chambersburg PA
CBHW060915250626
47159CB00008B/3018